Praise for the
award-winnin

M000074605

Dance of Desire
"On a scale of 1-5 stars, this is definitely a 6 star book!... Don't miss this one!"—6 stars, *Affaire de Coeur* Magazine

My Lady's Treasure
"Filled with lively characters, a strong, suspenseful plot and a myriad of romantic scenes *My Lady's Treasure* is a powerful, poignant tale."—5 stars and Reviewer's Choice Award, The Road to Romance

A Knight's Vengeance
"Kean (*Dance of Desire*) delivers rich local color and sparkling romantic tension in this fast-paced medieval revenge plot."—*Publishers Weekly*

A Knight's Temptation
"...an entertaining medieval romance brimming with sass, action, adventure, and lots of sexual chemistry."—*Booklist*

A Knight's Persuasion
...stirring adventure, superb characters, and enticing heroes. Ms. Kean continues to snag the reader with her fast-paced tales of heroic knights."—4-1/2 stars, *Affaire de Coeur* Magazine

A Knight and His Rose
"This is an ideal book for those looking for a quick afternoon read that will sweep them off their feet."—InDtale Magazine

A Witch in Time

by
Catherine Kean
and
Wynter Daniels

Published in the United States of America.

ISBN-10: 107338330X
ISBN-13: 978-1073383306
ASIN: B07T3RD4ZG

Cover design: Dar Albert, Wicked Smart Designs

Welcome to Cat's Paw Cove!

Dear Reader,

Cat's Paw Cove is a fictional, magical town where anything is possible! It was dreamed up by Wynter Daniels and Catherine Kean and is located south of St. Augustine on Florida's Atlantic coast. The name Cat's Paw Cove is derived from the small islands in the harbor, which look like the pads of a cat's paw.

We are so excited to bring you not only our own stories, but also contributions from an incredibly talented group of Guest Authors. With paranormal and mystery romances, historicals, time travels, and more, there's something for everyone.

We hope you'll enjoy reading the series as much as we enjoy writing it. For more information about the Cat's Paw Cove series, please visit:
http://CatsPawCoveRomance.com.

You are also welcome to join our fun, friendly Facebook group where you can interact with the authors, learn about our upcoming book releases and special events, and more:
https://www.facebook.com/groups/CatsPawCove/

Happy reading!

Wynter Daniels and Catherine Kean

Chapter One

*L*una opened her eyes and gazed up at an ominously black sky. Shivering against the damp wind, she tried to get her bearings.

Where am I?

And why was the ground moving? Not moving exactly, more like rocking. She inhaled and detected the salty smell of the sea. Propping herself up on her elbows, she scanned the surroundings. She was alone on the deck of an old-fashioned ship, like the one they'd raised from the harbor—which had been turned into the Shipwreck Museum.

The floorboards creaked nearby. Then she saw him—a man, leaning on the railing, facing the water. In the darkness, she could only make out his silhouette—a little taller than her brother Leo, and more broad-shouldered. The man's long hair blew around his face and neck, and his loose white shirt billowed in the wind. Gripping the railing, he turned his head her way.

Luna gulped, but knew immediately that he didn't see her. Still, she couldn't stop staring at him. He was...*ridiculously handsome.*

Only in my dreams....

She studied his strong jaw, chin, and cheekbones. His dark brows knotted. Until his eyes found Luna's, and his gaze trailed down her body, heating her skin as if he'd actually touched *her.*

Tendrils of desire spread through her.

Ding, ding, ding.

The unwelcome noise yanked her from the dream.

No! She hadn't even gotten to kiss him.

Ding, ding, ding.

She grabbed her phone from the nightstand and shut off the alarm. Squeezing her eyes closed, she tried to return to the ship, to the man.

A rough, wet tongue licked her chin.

"Meow?"

Luna groaned. "You're a poor substitute for my dream guy, Hecate."

The white cat with facial markings like a black mask around the eyes climbed onto Luna's chest and purred. And she knew from experience that Hecate wouldn't leave her alone until Luna fed her.

"Okay, fine." Luna eased Hecate off of her as she sat up in bed. It was almost 4:30, and she had to be at the café in half an hour to start the morning baking.

After pouring food into Hecate's bowl, she stumbled into the shower. Before she left for work, she knocked on the guest room door to wake her brother, who was staying with her after an epic fight with his girlfriend of the month. "Time to get up, Leo."

He grumbled something unintelligible.

"See you at seven," she said. "I fed Hecate. Don't believe her if she acts like she's hungry. And remember, Jordan and I will be leaving the café before nine for the Founders' Day event, so don't be late."

"Mm-hmm," he mumbled.

Founders' Day, ugh! It was going to be a long day, as it always was. But this year, aside from the crowds, period re-enactors, and all the vendors at the park to commemorate the seventeenth-century shipwreck that had led to the founding of Cat's Paw Cove, there was the additional draw of the preliminary opening of the Shipwreck Museum. Luckily, Cove Cat Café was only a ten-minute bike ride from her cottage near the beach—a little less at this time when the streets were virtually deserted. As she pedaled past Wilshire Park, the clock in the tower struck five.

She turned off of Whiskers Road into Calico Court then locked her bike on the rack next to the café door and let herself inside. When she switched on the lights, she glanced through the large window that separated the coffee shop from the cat room. A grey tabby yawned before returning to his nap. None of the other cats stirred.

Luna got right to work, baking enough cookies, pastries and miniature quiches for both the café and their Founders' Day booth. Three and a half hours flew past.

By the time Luna parked the work van behind their booth at Boardwalk Park, most of the other vendors were already set up. Good thing she had Jordan there to help her this year. Luna had a feeling that her very talkative friend and employee would make the day fly past.

The blonde chirped about her boyfriend, Sawyer. "...And he made the most amazing dinner last night." Jordan sighed. "I feel like the luckiest woman on the planet."

"That's great, sweetie." Luna climbed out of the van.

Jordan met her at the back of the vehicle. "My first Founders' Day." She helped Luna transfer cats from small carriers into the large pen at their booth on the boardwalk. "And the fact that it's such a special one—with the opening of the Shipwreck Museum—makes it even better! I'm so excited."

"Mm-hmm." Luna wished that she shared her friend's exuberance for the annual event. She probably should have asked her brother to handle the Cove Cat Café's vendor booth at the celebration, but Luna had always been the one to do it. Besides, she really was looking forward to the time with Jordan. In the short time she'd known the young woman, they'd become close friends. And Jordan's gift of communicating with animals had made the cat adoption part of the café run so much smoother. Hopefully, Jordan's bubbly personality would save Luna from having to engage with everyone who wanted to play with the cats, or hopefully, adopt one or two. Luna's naturally shy nature wasn't suited to working crowded festivals.

Who am I kidding?

The real reason she now hated Founders' Day had nothing to do with the hard work and long hours. But this year she had a plan. This morning she had cast a spell of protection around herself before she'd left the café. Too bad she hadn't thought to do that in years past. She'd have saved herself a whole lot of misery.

"Are you worried about the café?" Jordan asked. "I doubt it'll be busy today. Most of the town will be here. Leo can handle things there."

"I know." Luna had every confidence that her brother would be fine running the place by himself. So why was her stomach tied up in knots? Twice in the past three years, she'd met guys she'd ended up dating at Cat's Paw Cove's biggest yearly event. Both of those relationships had ended badly. But how could she have

CATHERINE KEAN and WYNTER DANIELS

known that Glen had had a fiancé in New York? He
certainly hadn't shared that information with her at any
point in the four months he and Luna had dated. Until
the woman had shown up at his door sporting a
suitcase and a canary diamond.

Then at last year's Founders' Day, Tim had
approached the Cove Cat Café's booth and played with
every cat in the pen. By the end of the day, he'd
convinced Luna to go out with him, against her better
judgment. He'd been so handsome and sweet. She
should have known that he'd been too good to be true.
The jerk had strung her along for three months before
admitting that he preferred men. He'd merely been
"trying to be straight" for his very-conservative
parents.

Yeah, she had a knack for choosing the most
unavailable guys. But this year she was safe. She was
taken, sort of. As soon as she really gave herself over
to the idea of dating Chuck, everything would be fine.

If only she could shake off that witchy
premonition that something was going to happen
today that would rock her world. No, it was probably
just the fact that she hadn't slept enough. She couldn't
get that strange dream of being on an old-fashioned
ship off her mind. And that insanely hot guy she'd seen
there. Must have been because of that news story she'd
seen on CPC-TV last night. Several members of the
Historical Society had spoken about the restoration of
the Guinevere. Luna had paid closer attention because
the reporter had interviewed one of Luna's regulars
from the café, Roberta Millingham.

The sheriff approached the booth and smiled
at Luna. "Good morning," he said. "Hi, Jordan."

"Hey, RJ," Jordan replied.

The sheriff stepped closer and lowered his voice. "I'm speaking to all the vendors before the festival kicks into high gear. I'd like you to let me know if anyone asks a lot of questions about the museum."

"What's going on, RJ?" Luna asked.

His lips flattened to a tight line. "I'm sure you've both heard the rumors that there's a secret treasure hidden somewhere on the ship. And believe me, I'm sure it isn't true. The restoration team has been all over that vessel. Ninety percent of it is completely restored. If there were any treasure to be found, they'd have come across it by now. But, there are still folks out there who think they can find what everyone else has missed."

"We'll call you if we hear or see anything suspicious." Jordan set a basket of cat toys for sale next to the bakery case chock full of Luna's homemade pastries and cookies. "How about a coffee, on the house?" She nudged Luna. "I'm sure my boss is down with that."

Luna grabbed a paper cup. "Absolutely. No sugar, extra cream, right?"

"You know me, Luna. Thanks." Sheriff Higgins grinned. "I hope you've got enough supplies for an army. I heard that ticket sales for today surpassed last year by more than fifty percent."

"Oh, great." Not! As she handed the sheriff his coffee, she glimpsed a crowd of festival-goers, some dressed up as pirates, headed her way. Swallowing, she mentally reinforced the protective shield around herself.

Atlantic Ocean, near St. Augustine, Florida
1645

"They're moving away," the ship's captain said, his spyglass trained on the vessel on the horizon.

Standing on the deck of the Guinevere beside the captain, Colin Wilshire released a sigh of relief, but the sound was snatched by the wind. The gentle sighing of the breeze had increased to an eerie whistling a short while ago when storm clouds had blackened the mid-afternoon sky.

Lightning flashed in the distance, accompanied by peals of thunder that were growing louder. The tempest was headed straight for them.

The storm must have convinced the other vessel—the captain believed it was a pirate ship—to change course.

Still frowning, the captain lowered his spyglass. Glancing over his shoulder, he shouted orders to his crew already working to adjust the sails. Other crewmembers on deck were tying ropes around barrels and nets to secure them.

Fifteen years older than Colin and with graying brown hair, the captain had made the journey from England to Barbados and back again four times. Before leaving the Port of London, he'd gathered all of the passengers together and had warned them of the risk of being attacked by buccaneers. Since families with young children were booked on the sailing, he'd felt an even greater responsibility to deliver the warning.

With Spanish galleons weighed down by riches traveling the waters, and the British also eager to claim a share of the New World's treasures, pirate attacks were a constant threat. The captain had offered to refund passengers' money if they decided they'd rather not make the sea journey, but no one had accepted the offer.

"It's good news, surely, that the pirates turned away?" Colin curled his right hand on the weathered rail and fought to keep his balance as the Guinevere rolled upon strong waves.

The captain shook his head. "Once the tempest is over, the pirates will be back."

"Perhaps their ship will be damaged in the storm. They might no longer be able to attack."

"It's possible." As Colin's hopes lifted a fraction, the captain added grimly, "Unfortunately, the marauders know these waters better than my crew and I. They know the islands and protected coves where they can drop anchor and wait out the storm. They know the reefs that can pierce a ship's hull. They'll let the wind and sea batter us. Then they will come for us."

Crikey. The situation couldn't possibly be so dire. "Can't we also seek shelter at one of those islands or coves?"

"And make it easy for the pirates to entrap us or force us aground? You must not have heard what pirates do to their captives."

Colin had indeed heard some harrowing tales. His cousin, Matthew Wilshire, who'd invested in a small shipping fleet that sailed from London to the Caribbean, had told him the stories after Colin had confided that he was going to leave England. "I wouldn't want anything to happen to you or your lovely wife," Matthew had said, his unusual, pale blue eyes lit with concern. "If I were you, I'd stay in England. I beg you, think about it."

Colin had, over many sleepless nights. Kept awake by his racing mind, he'd sat at the desk in his late father's study and had put quill and ink to parchment—rather ironic, when his sire had always considered Colin's creative pursuits a waste of time. Colin had finished the drawings of his latest invention; sketches he'd intended to show investors. He needed funds to not only make the wheeled contraption, but begin paying off his late father's secret, outstanding gambling debts. Colin had inherited them along with the bankrupt family estate and letters bearing King Charles I's official seal that demanded immediate payment of overdue taxes.

While Matthew had offered to loan Colin some money if he'd stay in the country, Colin couldn't accept. His cousin's finances were already at risk from investing in the fleet. Colin's sense of pride also wouldn't let him become indebted to anyone else, especially a widow with a limited income—his reason for refusing Evelyn's plea to borrow money from her mother. In the end, Colin had decided his only option was to use the savings he'd reserved for his inventions and flee. Perhaps in Barbados, once he and Evelyn were settled, he could look for investors.

In truth, Colin was already a hostage: of his late sire's financial ruin. Could being a prisoner of pirates really be as bad—or worse—than what he'd been facing in England?

As though following Colin's thoughts, the captain's scowl deepened. "The lucky captives of pirates are ransomed. The unlucky ones are sold as slaves or tortured for any bit of information that can be bartered for the buccaneers' gain. And the women…."

Colin thought of Evelyn in their cabin below deck.

"The women are used day and night until the pirates grow bored of them. Then they are sold or slain. Not, I vow, a fate you'd wish upon any of the fairer sex, let alone your wife who is carrying your babe."

"No." Imagining Evelyn facing such horrors made Colin's gut clench. While they hadn't wed for love—their fathers had arranged a marriage between them—he'd known her since they were children, and he cared about her. He had a responsibility to her, and he'd honor it until his dying breath.

If pirates did end up attacking the ship, he'd do all he could to protect her. Guilt grazed his heart, because it was, after all, his fault they were sailing to Barbados. His fault they were on the run and practically penniless. His fault she was lonely and miserable, as she'd reminded him every day since they'd left port.

As the wind rose to a hiss, and the Guinevere tilted hard to the left, Colin struggled to stay upright. Stinging raindrops began to fall from the heavens.

The helmsman, gripping the ship's wheel, shouted down to the captain then motioned to the water.

Colin glanced in the direction the helmsman had pointed, but could see only sea spray and churning waves.

"Go below," the captain said to Colin.

"Tell me how I can help." Colin didn't have much experience with ships, but since the Guinevere had set sail, he'd learned to tie knots, the basics of reading charts, and had fixed a window in the captain's cabin. "I realize you and your crew have sailed in storms before—"

"This is no ordinary storm."

The captain's words echoed Colin's own sense of dread. He'd experienced some strong thunderstorms in his lifetime, watched one recently from the leaded windows of the manor house he knew he was going to have to abandon. Yet, he'd never seen clouds as ominous as the ones overhead.

"Go below," the captain said again. "Stay with your wife."

Colin swiped away rainwater running down his face. "If you need my help—"

"I will call—"

The ship lurched to the left again. Men yelled over the hissing wind, while the soles of Colin's leather boots slipped on the deck and he careened into a post, pain jarring through his shoulder.

He steadied himself, to see the captain staggering toward the helmsman.

A wave crashed over the side of the vessel. Cold water sprayed over Colin, soaking his white linen shirt, and he gasped before grabbing hold of ropes nearby and making his way to the door and the cramped stairway that led to the cabins below.

As the ship groaned like a rusted gate, he stumbled down the hallway to his and Evelyn's room at the far end. Beyond the closed doors he passed, he heard frightened moans, worried voices, and crashes of objects hitting the floor. He'd met the Bells and Harrisons and most of the other passengers, and they were clearly terrified. There were cats on board too; Sherwoods, the captain had called them, a breed that had mask-like markings around their eyes. Two felines were huddled by his and Evelyn's cabin.

Colin thought to knock on the doors and

quickly check on the people inside—the captain and crew needed to focus on the ship, not the passengers—but when he heard a cry from the direction of his cabin, he hurried to see to Evelyn first.

He knocked twice then opened the door. The heat and stuffiness of the dark room hit him, along with a sour smell. Evelyn was clinging to the edge of the bunk, doubled over, her left arm wrapped around her belly. As the ship swayed and the door slammed inward against the cabin wall, she looked up. Tears streamed down her ashen face and onto her gown that even before the storm had badly needed washing.

"Colin—"

She threw up. As he stumbled into the room, following the cats that had darted inside, he saw more vomit on the floorboards. A pang of sympathy ran through him, because she'd already suffered for weeks from severe morning sickness. From the day they'd set sail, she'd been seasick. Being on the storm-ravaged boat must be utter hell for her.

Breathing hard, Evelyn dragged the back of her hand over her mouth. "I…can't stop…."

"It's all right." He managed to shut the door; the cats were now under the bolted-down chest of drawers, where they were welcome to stay. He lurched over to the bunk and on the way, snatched up their spare, clean chamber pot that had been sliding across the floor.

Evelyn squeezed her eyes shut. When she opened them again, tears welled along her bottom lashes. "We're going to die, aren't we?"

"Come now." He handed her the chamber pot, sat beside her, and put his arm around her waist. As he gripped the bunk to try and maintain his balance, he said, "The captain and crew—"

"They can't outwit nature." Her brown eyes blazed as she gestured to her rounded belly. "No one can."

He swallowed hard, wishing she hadn't brought their innocent, unborn babe into the discussion. Neither of them had expected her to get with child so soon after they'd married. It had happened so quickly, she must have conceived on their wedding night. But, a child—any child—was a miracle.

Colin very much looked forward to being a father. He'd vowed to be a far better parent than his own sire had been. Perhaps, if the child were a boy, he'd also be interested in inventing things. Surely Evelyn was excited to be a parent, despite their current predicament.

He stroked Evelyn's hair that was a rich brown color, like polished oak. She'd pinned it up earlier, but now most of her tresses tumbled to her lower back. "I spoke with the captain moments ago," Colin said. "We must trust his experience with storms—"

The ship rocked, and she groaned.

"—and you must trust me," he said.

She glared.

"Trust that I will protect and provide for you, as a responsible husband should." He sincerely meant those words. When Colin had asked about safekeeping important documents on the journey, the captain had told him that the Guinevere's former owner had been a smuggler; there was a secret cavity in the cabin Colin had booked. Colin had brought all of his sketches, protected by layers of canvas and stored inside a watertight wooden tube. After finding the secret spot concealed by crown molding, he'd hidden the tube in it.

Once they reached Barbados, he'd work hard to support Evelyn and not only the child they'd soon have, but any other offspring.

Moaning, she bent over the chamber pot.

He held her hair back from her face until she'd finished vomiting. Then he pulled the linen pillowcase from her pillow and handed it to her to wipe her mouth. He would have offered her water to rinse away the taste of bile, but the pitcher had fallen off the iron-bound trunk they'd used as a table and had shattered.

"I wish we'd never left England." Her words ended on a sob.

"Evelyn, we've talked about this."

"Don't you *dare* tell me to be quiet."

Colin gritted his teeth. "I wasn't going to. But—"

She averted her gaze. Her spine stiffened, and misgiving rippled through him. She was withholding something from him. Something important.

He gently squeezed with the arm around her waist. "What is it?" When she didn't answer, his misgiving deepened. "Are you hurt? Were you injured while you were alone?"

"No," she bit out.

He fought a welling of panic. "The babe. Is it all right?"

"As far as I can tell, it's fine." Tears dripped onto her bodice.

With an eerie creak, the ship listed to the right. She clutched the sloshing chamber pot with white-knuckled hands as he steadied them both.

The vessel finally leveled. The cabin, though, seemed to be growing smaller, closing in on Colin.

Sweat trickled down the back of his neck to blend with the seawater soaking his hair and shirt.

"I was going to wait to tell you," she said.

Bloody hell. He struggled to keep his voice steady. "Tell me what?"

She drew a sharp breath. "It's…it's about—"

A muffled *thud.*

The ship juddered.

As he and Evelyn were thrown several yards across the room, shouts and screams sounded down the hallway. The chamber pot flew from her hands and broke, its contents spreading over the floor.

"What's happened?" Evelyn cried, pushing up on one elbow.

"I don't know." She'd landed on her belly. His heart hammering, Colin struggled over to her. "How are you? Is the babe—?"

"We're all right," Evelyn said.

A muffled *crack*; the sound of splitting wood. Another *thud* that jolted the deck above their heads.

More urgent cries.

"I must go," Colin said.

"No." Wild-eyed, Evelyn caught his hand. "Stay with me. Please."

"I must do my part."

Her fingernails dug into his skin. "You'll abandon *me*? Our *child*?"

"No, I'm going to try and save you and everyone else on the ship. I promise, I'll return as soon as I can."

Chapter Two

Dear God.

The mainmast had snapped.

Braced in the doorway opening onto the deck, Colin watched in horror as the top half of the broken post, shattered but not severed, swung to and fro. The sail's tattered canvas whipped in the wind. The frayed ropes writhed like snakes.

Such damage would be hazardous to deal with on a calm, sunny day. With the wind howling and the rain being blasted sideways, getting lashed by one of the ropes would be deadly.

The mainmast, though, was clearly less urgent than another peril. Crewmen were looking over the side of the boat and yelling back at the captain.

Colin had passed several male passengers emerging from their cabins as he'd hurried to the stairs. He heard the men on the steps behind him, so he eased out onto the deck. The force of the wind and the rain made it hard to breathe, but he put his head down and grabbed onto whatever he could to make his way to the captain.

Lightning ripped apart the clouds overhead. Barrels, broken free from their ropes, rolled across the planks covered by streaming water. A dead crewman lay by the rail; the scruffy seafarer who had shared stories of his wild youth with Colin on several occasions. When the ship pitched and rocked, forcing Colin to tighten his grip on the tethered tender beside him, the corpse jostled then was lifted and washed away by a wave.

Seeing Colin, the captain yelled to him. The words, though, were indistinguishable.

"What did he say?" a passenger shouted from behind Colin.

"Don't know. Must get closer," Colin called back.

Thunder growled overhead, and another wave crashed onto the deck. With an ear-splitting *crack*, part of the nearest railing snapped. Floorboards splintered. Bits of wood and broken planks were carried off by the deluge racing toward the opposite side of the Guinevere.

Drenched, Colin spat out water and raked his sopping hair back from his face.

Lightning sizzled again.

A crewman, who'd just emerged from the doorway to the lower decks, gestured frantically to the captain. "...taking on water!" he screamed.

"What?" Colin bellowed.

Glancing at Colin, the crewman spread his arms wide. "...hole...hull."

They must have hit a reef.

"...going to sink," the man shouted.

As icy fear whipped through Colin, the captain met his gaze. His jaw clenched, the older man pointed to the tenders.

The ship suddenly tilted. The captain, knocked

off his feet, fell to the deck. A barrel slammed into his chest. He cried out in agony.

"No!" Colin choked.

Crew members scrambled to reach their leader, but another wave rushed in. Caught in the fast-moving water, the captain fought to keep his head up as he was swept away.

"What do we do now?" another passenger called from behind Colin.

Fear became a brutal knot in Colin's chest. The captain was gone, perhaps drowned, and the ship was sinking. Their chances of surviving the storm were slim.

Evelyn and their baby might die.

Never. He'd promised to protect her; he wouldn't break his promise.

Some of the crew had obviously decided to abandon the Guinevere, because they'd begun untying the longboat farther down the deck. Squinting against the pounding rain, Colin looked back at the other men. "We'll take boats, too."

"Madness!" another passenger yelled. "We'll never survive the waves."

"We don't have a choice," Colin shouted back, rainwater streaming into his mouth. He gestured to the gray-haired gentleman nearest the door. "Get the women and children. *Go!*"

The wide-eyed passenger, clearly close to panic, disappeared down the stairs.

Colin motioned to several other men. "Help me." They worked together to try and untie the nearest boat. Another passenger handed Colin a knife, and he sawed at a rope.

He thought of his sketches in the cabin. He

mustn't forget them. Once the women and children were in the tenders, he'd run down and retrieve the tube before getting into a boat himself.

His fingernails blue, his hands shaking, Colin continued to cut the rope. It wasn't easy, when the Guinevere dipped, rocked, and they kept getting knocked off their feet.

Finally, the rope began to fray.

"Colin!" His head snapped up at Evelyn's voice.

He straightened to see her in the doorway. One of the young Bell daughters, crying and hugging a cloth doll, stood close behind her.

He handed the knife to the man beside him then struggled across the deck to Evelyn.

"I'm so frightened," she sobbed.

"Hold onto me," he said close to her ear. "I'll help you—"

The boat pitched violently.

Thrown sideways, Evelyn shrieked.

Colin's left arm instinctively went around her, barely keeping her from falling face down on the deck. With his right, he caught the screaming girl.

As he staggered, trying not to fall himself, a huge wave crashed over the rail. Barrels, ropes, and sections of plank were sucked into the turgid water. The wave swirled toward Colin and the other passengers, who were shouting in alarm.

No, Colin silently cried. *Please. No!*

Even as he shielded his wife with his body, he knew there was nothing he could do. The deluge slammed into them, and he lost his hold on Evelyn and the girl. As he was sucked backward into the wave, he collided with another passenger and some debris.

Pain seared through Colin's skull.

Through the agony, he realized he'd been pulled underwater.

Coldness.

Distorted gurgling sounds.

Bits of wood bumped against him. His elbow hit something solid—the rail?—before the wave's momentum sent him into the ocean.

Lightning flickered, illuminating the water's surface above him. As though trapped in a nightmare, he saw the hulking silhouette of the Guinevere to his left. Debris slowly sank in the water.

His lungs burned for air, but the undertow yanked him down, down into the inky depths.

He was going to drown.

No!

Evelyn. Oh God, Evelyn.

He forced his cold, numb arms to move and his legs to kick. Slowly, he rose, twisting to avoid sinking objects. With the surface in sight, he kicked as hard as he could. His head broke through the churning water, and he gasped for breath, filling his lungs an instant before a wave swamped him.

Coughing out seawater, his eyes and nose streaming, he drew in several more breaths then swam to a broken plank and hung onto it. On the next wave, he saw a cat struggling to stay afloat. He kicked his way over to it and pulled it onto the end of his board, where it huddled, weary and soaked.

Catching his breath, he squeezed his eyes shut. When he used his sleeve to wipe away the water dripping down his face, blood stained the linen. But, he wouldn't rest until he'd found Evelyn. He prayed she wasn't hurt, and that their baby hadn't come to harm. There had to be other passengers in the water who'd need help, too.

Thunder snarled, followed by bright streaks of lightning. More boards bobbed on the water a short distance away.

"Help," a woman cried, her voice distorted by the wind. "Please, someone help me."

"Evelyn?" he shouted.

"Help!" the woman called again, and he headed toward the sound.

He found her, coughing and spluttering. She wasn't his wife, but Mrs. Harrison. When their gazes met, an exhausted sob broke from her.

"I've got you," he said, slipping his arm around her waist. Her shoulders slumped in relief.

A broken plank bumped against her, and she reached for it, but he grabbed hold of a larger section of boards and pulled it closer. "Hold onto this with all your might."

"Thank you. You're bleeding—"

"I'll be all right. Have you seen anyone else in the water?"

Mrs. Harrison shook her head.

"I must find my wife."

The woman sobbed. "Please don't let me go."

He had to.

"I'll come back," he said, "once I've found Evelyn. Climb up onto the board. That way you can save your strength."

He coaxed Mrs. Harrison up onto the makeshift raft. As the wind shrieked over the angry water, she shivered. "Hold on," he shouted.

A loud thud sounded behind Colin. He glanced over his shoulder, but the biting wind blurred his vision.

A hard object slammed into his head.

Pain.

His eyelids fluttered.

You must stay awake. Find Evelyn....

Blackness.

Jordan handled most of the folks interested in the cats while Luna sold the food and drinks, just as they did at the café. Jordan wowed people with her uncanny ability to match prospective clients with the best kitty for them. Of course, Luna knew it was because Jordan could talk to the animals and get their feedback.

A Founders' Day re-enactor—a redheaded guy dressed in pirate garb—stopped a few feet from the booth and slipped on mirrored sunglasses, which totally blew his pirate look.

"Cool shades," Luna said to him.

Frowning at her, he said, "What?"

She pointed to his glasses. "I don't think they had sunglasses in the seventeenth century."

He squared his shoulders, glaring at her. "Why is that your business?"

Whoa. Luna held up her hands in surrender. "Forget I mentioned it."

Thankfully, the man hurried away. She contemplated calling the sheriff since the guy's behavior had been a little weird, but she was probably overreacting.

Before she could think more about it, a middle-aged couple approached the booth and oohed and aahed over a Siamese cat. "Is she spayed?" the man asked Jordan.

Jordan shook her head. "*He* is neutered." She took the feline out and handed him to the woman. "His name is Sinbad, and he prefers to be an only cat, although he wouldn't mind living with another adult cat. Just no dogs, please."

The man laughed. "Did he tell you that?"

The cat surely had told Jordan what he wanted.

Jordan went on. "I just found him a few days ago. He'll make a great pet."

Luna snickered and pointed past the boardwalk arcades to the lighthouse in the harbor. "She's a lot like that beacon, but for stray cats."

"That's true," her friend agreed.

When the couple wouldn't commit to the adoption, Jordan moved on to another potential family, one with a few small kids. And after wowing the children with her ability to read the felines' thoughts—something that the parents no doubt assumed was a parlor trick—Jordan managed to place two kittens with the family.

"You're great at that," Luna told her after the family had left.

"My gift has come in handy," Jordan said. "How do you think I convinced Sawyer to propose to me? I persuaded his cat to lead him to his grandmother's engagement ring as a hint."

Luna gasped. "No way."

Jordan chuckled. "Just kidding. But seriously, I did help him solve a pretty big mystery right after we met."

"That's...amazing. How'd you do that?"

Jordan waited until a few event-goers had passed before she spoke. "Well, I'm sure you read in the *Cat's Paw Cove Courier* that his aunt tried to have him killed and then stole Sawyer's share of the Sherwood House."

Luna remembered the story, which had been big news last year. Sawyer's Aunt Angelica had been one of the wealthiest and most prominent residents of the town. Her arrest had been a huge shock to everyone. "Sure, but I didn't realize that you'd helped make that happen."

A proud smile settled on Jordan's face. "Actually, Angelica's Doberman told me that he remembered Angelica and her late husband arguing about killing someone. That someone turned out to be Sawyer. Thank goodness they'd failed at murder."

"Holy cow."

Jordan nodded. "He was living up in Georgia. Sawyer had no idea who he really was. You see, he had amnesia from someone hitting him on the head. His cat led us back here."

Luna had heard bits and pieces of the tale, but until that moment, she hadn't put it all together.

Hours later, as the sun sank low on the horizon, Luna and Jordan returned to the café with three fewer cats and just a handful of leftover pastries.

Luna was completely wiped out, yet relieved that her spell of protection had apparently worked. Not a single guy had hit on her. Finally, she let down her guard. Keeping her spiritual shield in place had sapped her energy. She thanked Jordan for her help with the event and made sure that her brother was okay closing the café by himself.

"Go home, sis," Leo insisted. "Take a nap. I

know you didn't get much rest last night. You were moaning in your sleep. I heard you all the way in my room."

Face heating, she said, "Sorry about that."

Leo nodded as he wiped down the counter. "Go, get out of here."

"Thanks." Luna pressed a kiss to his cheek. "See you later."

Minutes later, she arrived home at the cottage and plopped down on the overstuffed chair in the living room. The soothing sound of the waves in the distance lulled her into a dreamy state.

A tempest howled all around her. The blackest sky she'd ever seen threatened to engulf her as the ship rocked in the stormy sea. Wooden boards creaked and moaned. Then snapped with an explosive pop.

The ship was breaking apart. It was only a matter of time. Luna's breath locked in her chest.

Was she going to die?

Before she could figure that out, a giant wave swallowed her up and dumped her into the cold ocean. Debris cluttered the surface. She pumped her legs to stay afloat. Spitting out the salty swill in her mouth, she gasped for breath. She wouldn't last much longer.

A male voice reached through her panic. "I've got you."

A strong arm slipped around her waist. The man drew her against his body. She had but a moment to look at his face— her hero—before her limbs went limp, sapped of all strength. Thank goodness for the man.

Something bumped her right side—a broken plank. She grabbed onto it and uttered her thanks to the universe.

"That one's better." The man reached for a larger section of boards to her left, and hauled it closer. "Hold onto this with all your might."

He was going to release her. Fresh panic drummed through her. "Please don't let me go."

Ignoring her plea, he helped her onto the makeshift raft. "Hold on," he shouted.

A piece of debris came out of nowhere, hitting the man's head. His eyes fluttered for a second before he slipped under the water.

She tried to grab him, but he'd disappeared into the black depths.

"Come back!" she screamed. Too late. He was gone. "No!"

She startled awake. In her quiet living room. She was dry, warm.

If only she could return to that dream, that man. She couldn't get her handsome hero's face off her mind.

His eyes were a deep mahogany. His square jaw and straight nose appeared to have been carved from granite. And that voice—so sure and deep—had calmed her through the ordeal. But had he survived?

It was only a dream.

The man had been so real. So heroic.

She should have known that the only place she'd have found such a great, good-looking guy was in her imagination. *Real* men lied and cheated, presented themselves as single when they weren't. Except for one.

Chuck. Why couldn't she just get on board with the notion of a relationship with the man? He had it all—a great job as a number cruncher for the city of Jacksonville, a beautiful home near the beach. Chuck was perfect boyfriend material. Most importantly, he came without any drama or old baggage. She'd only known him for a few months, so maybe that was the problem. She merely needed time to build an attraction for him, which was surely why she couldn't bring herself to encourage him in his pursuit of her, at least not yet.

Hecate pounced on her stuffed mouse under the coffee table. Then the feline picked up the toy and dropped it at Luna's feet.

Luna threw the mouse across the room, and just as she always did, Hecate went to retrieve it. "Don't you know that this is a dog's game, not a cat's?"

Hecate pawed the toy, moving it even closer to Luna.

"Fine." She threw it into the hallway as she stood up. "We'll play more later, Hecate. Mommy needs some beach therapy." Yes, she relished a little time to herself. Her go-to self-care treatment was always a long walk near the shore.

Grabbing a light shawl and her keys, she headed out. By the time she reached the beach, the calm skies had clouded up, turning the gold sunset a hundred shades of pink, purple and gray. She glanced toward the boardwalk, surprised to see a lot of people still there. The festival should have been winding down by now. Perhaps the Shipwreck Museum was still open and attracting interested tourists.

Thunder boomed in the distance. Luna's skin tingled.

Storms didn't usually frighten her. She'd grown up in a hurricane zone, but this one made her a little nervous. She pulled her shawl tighter around her shoulders as she neared her favorite spot—a narrow strip of beach below the highest dunes, close to the entrance to several of the area's underground tunnels. Sitting on the sand, she breathed in the soothing salt air, listened to the waves lap at the shore. Even in the rain, the spot was so peaceful, her safe haven.

Suddenly, a menacing figure staggered out from behind a rock—right toward her.

Indecision paralyzed her. Perhaps he'd pass her without incident. But when she realized he was heading straight toward her, it was too late to bolt.

Swallowing hard, Luna closed her hand around a chunk of driftwood on the beach and steeled herself. "Get back," she shouted. But the man kept coming.

Illuminated only by moonlight, the guy looked like some kind of monster as he drew closer—seaweed hung from his wet hair, debris covered his clothes. In this town full of all sorts of paranormal beings, anything was possible, although her witchy senses didn't pick up on any supernatural energy from the guy. He was most likely a re-enactor, like the guy with the sunglasses earlier. This man had probably had too much to drink.

Pointing toward the Shipwreck Museum, he dropped to his knees. "It's the Guinevere!"

"Yep, that's the Guinevere."

"My ship," he said in a very convincing British accent.

Okay, so he wasn't a monster, just a lunatic. Which made him infinitely more dangerous. And he appeared to be injured. Blood ran down the side of his face from the long gash on his forehead. Was it real or just part of his costume?

Luna inched away from him, fearful for her safety.

Until she got a better look at his clothes—the loose-fitting white shirt with voluminous sleeves, knee-length pants that buttoned up the sides. She pulled her cell out of her back pocket and turned on the flashlight, training it on the man.

Recognition hit her like a slap of icy air, and her fear abated. Her dream man! How could that be?

"What magic is this?" He shielded his face from the light. "Are you a mermaid? Or a sea nymph? I've heard sailors speaking of such creatures."

If he was a re-enactor, he certainly was staying in character. The injury on his forehead looked real enough, though. "Are you hurt?" She reached out to touch the wound, but he backed away.

"Stay away," he ground out. "I know what you are, witch! Any closer, and you'll surely steal my breath."

Well, she was a witch, of course, but not the kind he seemed to think. "I won't hurt you," she assured him.

He slid farther away. "Why are your braids blue then, like a mermaid's hair?"

Luna stifled a chuckle. "It's just dyed."

The man got to his feet. "I don't believe you. I won't be lured by your beauty."

Her beauty? Clearly, his head injury had affected his mind. "Why don't you let me take you to the boardwalk? I saw a medic station there earlier today. Maybe it's still open."

Narrowing his eyes at her, he stood his ground.

She held up her hands in surrender. "My name is Luna. I don't mean you harm. Let me help you."

The man kept glancing toward the Shipwreck Museum then back at her. Did he really think that the raised ship was his? When he didn't speak for several moments, Luna racked her brain to think of a way to convince him to go with her.

"What's your name?" she asked.

He hesitated before answering. "Colin."

Okay, that was a start. "Would you at least follow me to the nurse? Your head wound should be looked at."

"I must find my wife. She was on the ship with me."

Luna gasped. Images of her dream filled her head—being on a ship's deck in a bad storm, her dream man's face—this man. How could it be? Her head buzzed with questions.

Wait, he'd just mentioned that he was married. The notion shouldn't bother her. "Your wife?"

Colin nodded. "Evelyn is with child. And she was ill."

Worse—a pregnant wife. Who was probably worried sick about her husband. "Would you like me to call her for you?"

Colin gave Luna a blank stare. "I'm quite sure she won't hear you."

Yeah, that head wound had done some damage. Returning her phone to her pocket, she motioned for Colin to follow her. "Please, we need to get you some medical help."

He folded his arms over his chest. "I'm sorry, but I won't succumb to your siren song. I fear you're luring me to a witch doctor. I'll not go."

Chapter Three

Colin returned the blue-haired vixen's glower, even as he fought not to collapse in the sand. His head pounded, and exhaustion weighed upon him like a leaden blanket. What he would give to be able to lie down, close his eyes, and sleep for a while. Even his hard bunk on the ship would be heavenly—although last he remembered, the vessel had hit a reef and had been breaking to pieces.

How then, could he see the Guinevere now, with its posts and sails seemingly intact? The ocean, too, wasn't churning but calm, as if the tempest hadn't taken place.

What had happened to him? Had he died? If so, this wasn't anything like the Heaven he'd expected.

Had he swallowed too much sea water? Had his brain coddled in his skull and he'd gone mad? Fear accompanied a shrill ringing sound in his ears.

"Hey." Luna touched his arm. "Don't pass out on me."

"Pass…what?"

"There's no way I can drag you down the beach or carry you to the medic station."

Colin frowned as his gaze raked over her. That,

at least, was the truth. She was far too petite to bear his weight. Nicely formed, he'd already noticed, despite her shawl-like covering and odd garments underneath. Such clothing must be the traditional garb worn by colonists in this area.

Still, why would she believe he'd want to be dragged down the beach or carried? Was that customary when folk encountered other people they didn't know? Perhaps it was required by the officials of the so-called medic station.

The last thing he needed was more sand in his arse, but he didn't want to cause offense.

"Don't get upset," Luna said in a soothing tone. "I really do want to help you."

God help him, but he wasn't the only one who needed help. "Evelyn—"

"You can tell the medics what happened to you. They'll know who to contact," Luna added. "They might be able to get a search started for her."

That did, indeed, sound like a good plan.

"Also, see those lights out there?" Luna pointed to the water. "They're from boats. The folks on one of them might have already found Evelyn."

His heart leapt, even as he recalled helping Mrs. Harrison onto the makeshift raft before he'd blacked out. "Evelyn's not the only one. There are others."

"How many others?"

He tried to recall the faces of the other passengers. "There were at least fifteen of us—men, women, and children—not including the captain and crew. If others survived, they may be injured too."

Luna studied him. "You were on a fairly large boat, then."

He gestured to the ship. "That large."

She exhaled a heavy sigh. "Okay, just so we're clear…. You're involved with the local Historical Society, right?"

"What Historical Society?"

"The one that organized the re-enactment of the shipwreck. Isn't that why you're in costume?"

Colin nearly choked. "You think I am part of an *act*?"

Her grip tightened on her shawl. "I'm not sure what to believe. I'd like to understand what's going on here."

"As would I." Impatience gnawed. "I swear, there was a terrible storm. The ship hit a reef. I witnessed the vessel breaking apart, men being washed overboard." Colin almost couldn't bear to remember, but he must, in order to get help.

"How did you get from the ocean to this beach?"

An excellent question; one he couldn't answer. "I'm…not sure. Nor can I explain why the tempest has vanished. But, as far as I know, I'm the only one who reached shore." He gestured to the water. "The rest must still be out there."

Luna's gaze shifted to the calm expanse of sea then back to him. "Colin, I'm going to ask you an important question, and you need to answer me truthfully."

"I've spoken the truth from the moment we met," he gritted.

Her throat moved with a swallow. "Did you have a few drinks tonight?"

"I drank a lot of seawater—"

"I meant wine. Liquor—"

"*No!*"

She hesitated then asked, "Are you and the others you mentioned…illegal aliens?"

What the hell were ayleeuns? Not just any old ayleeuns, but *illegal* ones?

Colin's pulse quickened because while he didn't fully understand her question, he did know what illegal meant. Fleeing England to escape his inherited debts would most certainly be considered illegal. If he was arrested in this foreign land, he might be separated from Evelyn for months or even years. He might even be sent back to England for sentencing.

He wouldn't be able to protect Evelyn, wouldn't see his newborn child or be able to help raise it. "I…well…." The ringing noise sounded in his ears again.

Luna squeezed his arm, pulling his focus back to the moonlit beach. "It's okay. We don't have to talk about that now."

Thank God.

Luna sighed again. "Whatever's happened to you, I am still going to help you. Your wife and the others, too."

Relief rushed through him. He almost sank to his knees.

"You'll need to come with me, though. It's a bit of a walk."

At least she hadn't insisted on dragging or carrying him. He nodded, even as he resolved to keep his wits about him. If she'd planned to trick him, or if officials tried to arrest him, he'd be ready.

Luna started walking, and he fell in beside her. He'd lost his boots to the ocean, so sand pushed up between his toes that were already gritty with sand. Now and again, Colin stepped on hard things he couldn't see—hopefully seashells and not creatures with sharp teeth and pointy spines that would pierce through the soles of his feet and feast on his flesh, or something equally ghastly.

"What land is this, if you don't mind my asking?" he said.

Luna glanced at him, but didn't slow her pace. "The United States."

He'd never heard of such a place.

"You're from England, right?"

"Aye." No point denying it. He had an upper-class British accent and wouldn't be able to convincingly replicate the way she spoke even if he tried.

"I want to take a vacation there someday." She sounded wistful. "I've seen pictures of the landscape and old castles there, and think it must be very picturesque."

Sadness tugged at his soul as he thought of the estate he'd been forced to abandon. "It is indeed picturesque, especially in winter when the ground and trees are covered with snow."

She shivered. "I don't like snow."

He thought of the afternoon he'd had to help Matthew free his carriage from icy ruts in the dirt road. That incident had sparked ideas for Colin's latest invention, although he had no idea if his sketches had survived the storm. At some point, he must find out. "Snow does make traveling difficult," he finally said. "It's not a good time to visit England now, though. Not with the civil unrest. Our King—"

"You mean Queen."

A new monarch had claimed the English throne? Being at sea, he hadn't heard the news.

"Careful. There are steps ahead," Luna said.

"Right." Colin looked to where she'd pointed, but bright lights drew his gaze higher.

What in hell…?

Evenly spaced and running in a line, tall metal posts ended in oval-shaped orbs that were larger than his head. There seemed to be other sources of light as well. Some were moving, their lights glaring for a short moment and then fading. There were odd sounds, too, mingled with the noise of crowds of people talking and laughing: honks and rumblings that didn't sound at all like horse-drawn carriages.

"Come on." Luna's footsteps thudded on the wooden stairs up toward the lights.

Panic raced through Colin. For a moment, there were too many strange, new things to think about. He longed to turn and run back down the beach, but he wasn't a coward. Nor must he delay getting help for Evelyn and the others who'd survived the shipwreck.

He followed Luna up to an open area surrounded by planks and rails. He glanced about, his senses on high-alert. A lot of folk, most in similar garb to Luna, were standing or sitting in the area fringed by shops and, judging by the smell, places to get cooked food.

His gaze fixed on several men walking toward them, and his jaw clenched.

Pirates.

Were they men from the ship the captain had seen before the storm hit?

He grabbed Luna's arm. "Beware."

"Colin!"

He pulled her in close. "Pirates," he hissed

against her ear. Her hair smelled of flowers. A really nice smell—

"Of course there are pirates." She faced him, looking bemused. "People are dressed up for the Founders' Day celebrations, just like you are."

The buccaneers approached, their carefree, swaggered strides clearly part of a well-rehearsed deception. They wanted their victims to believe they weren't under any threat, in order to get close and take them hostage. Luna must not be aware of the vile things pirates did to others. Colin's hand flexed, for he wished he had his sword to wield. He'd send a warning that the bastards shouldn't come any closer to him or Luna.

One of the men, ginger-haired and with the straightest teeth Colin had ever seen, grinned at her.

Colin growled.

"Stop," she muttered.

"I will *not* allow them to take you captive."

"Take me…?"

"Do you not know how pirates use their female prisoners?"

As the men strode past, Luna rolled her eyes. "Good thing I'm not interested in any of those guys. If I'd hoped for a date with one of them, you ruined my chances."

Colin snorted. He didn't quite understand what sweet, oval-shaped dates had to do with her and pirates, but he'd ponder that later. "Is the medic station close by?"

"Yes. This way."

He walked with her through the crowd, while planning how he'd handle the medical care. If he was taken inside a building, he'd be sure to note the ways out, in case he needed to get away fast. He didn't have any money on him—all that he'd had was on the storm-battered ship—and there would be a cost to having his injuries tended. No gentleman would allow a woman to pay for him, and he already owed Luna for helping him. Perhaps he could barter for the medical help, or—

He startled at a booming roar followed by a rhythmic thumping and cacophony of sound. He'd never heard such musical instruments before. Through a gap in the crowd, he saw the source of the noise: a shiny, black box on wheels with bright lights on the front. There were boxes of other styles and colors, too, lined up together.

He gestured to the black box, now moving backward. "What's that?"

"A souped-up Mustang, I think."

Souped up…? Colin forced down the question. There were other people close by who might overhear and become suspicious of him. Also, the box had moved out of sight, and Luna was heading toward a large tent with a red cross on the side—the medic station.

His strides slowed as he took in the interior of the tent: a chair that was covered in thin, white parchment and looked like it could be adjusted to form a bed; a table with gauze and some odd-looking instruments that reminded him of torture devices.

A woman a little shorter than Luna turned, saw Luna, and they started talking.

Shock and unease gripped him. The woman's corseted blouse revealed an astonishing amount of cleavage, and her dress….

He blinked. Shook his head.

Luna returned to him. "You okay?"

A muscle ticked in his jaw. He drew Luna to one side so the other woman wouldn't hear. "What is the meaning of this?" he hissed.

Luna frowned. "I don't—"

"You bring me to a…a…."

Her brows rose. "A?"

"A pirate wench?"

"Um…."

"A *strumpet*?"

Luna made a strangled snorting noise. Obviously trying not to laugh, she pressed her hand over her mouth.

"This isn't funny," he bit out.

"Oh, yeah, it is."

"I am most certainly not in the mood to…." Colin waved his hand, lost for words. He'd never imagined discussing fornication with a woman he barely knew.

Luna snorted again. "Why do guys think about sex all the time?"

"Not true." He didn't think about it when he was asleep. He hadn't once thought about it during the tempest. But, that raised another question. "Do your people believe coupling has healing powers? That it can mend wounds?"

Luna squeezed the bridge of her nose and groaned. "Just be quiet for a moment, okay?"

He scowled. He didn't want to be quiet. He wanted to get his injury tended and find Evelyn. But, he couldn't do those things without Luna's help, so he nodded.

"First of all, she's not a pirate wench or a strumpet. She's an RN."

"RN?"

"A registered nurse."

He grunted. "Registered in torture?"

"What? No!"

"What, exactly, does she nurse?"

Luna appeared to be struggling for patience. "She's here to treat people who get injured during the Founders' Day festivities. She told me she just finished treating a man who'd sprained his ankle during the Pirate Pub Crawl."

Pirate Pub Crawl? How many damned pirates were there in this area?

Colin's gaze slid to the wench, who was standing by the chair and table of torture devices. She smiled at him. A friendly enough smile, but she could well be trying to lure him in.

That ringing noise sounded in his ears again.

"Colin," Luna said. "I promise, she'll help you, not hurt you. There might be a bit of discomfort when she cleans your wound—"

"What if I don't want her help?"

Luna shook her head. "I can deal with cuts and bruises, but a gash to the head? No. And frankly, I don't want to be responsible for your care when I don't have the skills."

A plea shone in Luna's eyes. It was important to her that he got help from the wench.

"Fine," he said quietly "But if I sense she's trying to trick me, I will immediately leave."

"You'll also be polite and not once use the word 'strumpet.' Agreed?"

He had to trust Luna's greater experience in such situations. "Agreed."

Colin walked with Luna into the tent.

"That's quite a wound." The wench eyed his brow. "What happened?"

"Shipwreck," he said.

"Ri-ight." She winked. "I get it. We're staying in character."

"In…?" He glanced at Luna, who shook her head: a silent warning that he should just agree with what had been said.

"Aye," he said. "Why not? These are the Founders' Day festivities, after all."

The woman laughed and motioned him toward the chair.

He squared his shoulders. "First, I must tell you about the others."

"Others?"

"From the shipwreck."

The woman's puzzled gaze shifted to Luna.

"We must rescue them. I know there are boats out on the water, but—"

"Let's check you over first, okay?" the wench said. "You can't be of help to anyone else if you're not in good shape yourself."

He had no idea how his 'shape' was at all relevant, but he reluctantly nodded his agreement and approached the chair. Was he supposed to sit on the parchment? Or was he to write a list of his aches and pains on it? He'd need a quill and ink, but couldn't see either by the chair or on the table.

"Just have a seat," the wench instructed.

Colin sat, becoming aware of discomfort in his torso and legs that he hadn't acknowledged before. Beneath him, the parchment crinkled; a fascinating sound. He shifted to the left and right several times, just to hear the crinkle. Luna shook her head again, more vigorously this time. Why did she look like she wanted to slap him?

The wench handed him a board with more sheets of parchment. These were different than the parchment upon which he sat. Marveling at the smoothness and thinness, he rubbed the pages between his thumb and forefinger.

"You need to fill them out." The nurse handed him a strange-looking quill. "Name, address, regular doctor's information and—"

"I don't have it." Meeting the nurse's gaze, he shrugged. "It was on the ship."

"Oh. I see." The pirate wench winked again. "I'm guessing you don't have medical insurance?"

"I'll pay," Luna said.

"No. I can't allow that." Colin said.

"It's the way things need to be done," Luna answered firmly.

Ah. Another thing he'd be wise to just agree to. He nodded, but he'd make sure he repaid her for the cost of his treatment.

The woman picked up a black object from the table. Part of it was bulbous; another part looked like it was meant to wrap around and constrict a limb. Is that what was going to happen?

"I'm going to start by taking your blood pressure," the wench said, as though aware of his concern. "My digital monitor broke, so I have to do this the old-fashioned way."

He tensed as she reached for his arm. He didn't want to look the fool, but he'd never had the pressure of his blood taken before. Did it hurt? Where was she going to put that bulbous thing?

Grinning, the nurse pushed up his damp

sleeve. "Don't worry. If you sit still and behave like a gentleman, I won't make you walk the plank."

Luna waited as the medic cleaned Colin's head wound.

"Well, his neurological responses are fine—vision, hearing, balance, etc." The woman faced Luna and shrugged. "I don't think he understands what century he's in, though."

Luna nodded. "Could that be from the injury?"

"Maybe. Just to be on the safe side, I'd suggest taking him over to the hospital for a CT scan." She carefully applied Steri-Strips to the side of Colin's forehead. "Could just be that the guy is a time traveler from a few hundred years ago. You never know, right?"

Luna chuckled. "Yeah, sure."

"You'll want to keep a close eye on him for the next twenty-four hours. Rest is important."

The medic helped Colin sit up. "Thank you for finally allowing me to treat you."

He gave the woman a wary frown. "I didn't know that pirate wenches were so skilled in healing."

The medic snickered then touched Luna's arm. "Are you parked nearby, hon?"

"I live close," Luna assured her as they left the tent. She tried to take Colin's arm, but he nudged her away. "I must find my ship now, or what's left of it. Evelyn needs me." He fell in step with Luna. "Where are you going?"

"First, we have to go to the hospital." She

stepped off the boardwalk and onto the beach. "It's too far for you to walk, especially in your condition. After we get you checked out, I'll help you find your wife, okay?"

That seemed to satisfy him for the moment. Until he gasped. "What magic is this?"

Luna followed his gaze to a jet as it flew overhead.

"It's just an airplane."

Colin shook his head. "This is a strange land with its moving stars and blinking candles."

Luna huffed. "Are you for real?"

"Pardon?"

She folded her arms over her chest. "I get the whole method acting thing, immersing yourself in the role, but you can drop it now. It's just the two of us."

Colin furrowed his brow. "My lady, I'm unsure of what you mean. Need I remind you that I am the one who finds myself shipwrecked in this place. I must find my wife. She could be hurt. We have to organize a search party right away."

For goodness sake. How long was Colin going to stay in character? "So, what year was it when this supposedly happened?"

"1645, of course."

"Okay," she said. "Whatever you say. Just to be clear, there was a shipwreck here in 1645. The Guinevere sank near the shore of the largest island in the harbor. But if this Evelyn person was on the ship, I kind of doubt that she's still out there. It's been more than three hundred and seventy years since then. There's nothing that you or a search party can do for her now."

"Three hundred and seventy years...." His

voice trailed off, and he swayed a little, so Luna took hold of his arm. "Are you all right?"

Colin remained silent. He sure didn't look okay. Even in the dark, she could see that his complexion had paled.

The nurse's jest replayed in Luna's mind.

"Could just be that the guy is a time traveler from a few hundred years ago. You never know, right?"

Colin rubbed his eyes. "We were bound for Barbados when the storm hit." He sighed, and his shoulders sank. "Evelyn hadn't wanted to leave England."

"Why not?"

Hanging his head, he mumbled something under his breath. "I insisted."

"Were the two of you traveling alone?"

"Alone? Of course not. There were other families on board—the Bells, the Harrisons…."

The Bells and Harrisons? Luna was quite familiar with those names since they belonged to two of the founding families of the town, and their descendants still lived in Cat's Paw Cove. "What's your full name?"

He straightened. "Colin Wilshire."

Wilshire? Another founding family. Luna's head buzzed with questions. Could he possibly be for real?

Her heart raced. She recalled the two dreams in which she'd seen him. The ship had been like something out of a pirate movie. What if he really was from the past? How could she know? She racked her brain to think of a way to test him. "Who's the current British monarch?"

"King Charles, of course."

Taking out her phone, she Googled her question. Colin was right. King Charles the first had held the throne in 1645. "And who was the king before him?"

"His father, King James. He'd been King James VI of Scotland before he'd inherited the throne of England after Queen Elizabeth died."

Luna quickly checked the facts. Colin was correct. Either he was a delusional history wiz, or he'd actually lived several centuries ago. The possibility stole her breath away.

Maybe the best thing to do was just take him to the hospital, as the nurse had suggested, and quietly ask the doctor to do a psychological evaluation on him. She set a gentle hand on Colin's arm. "I'm going to drive you to the hospital."

His brow furrowed. "The hospital?"

"A bigger medical place than the tent we just left."

"Absolutely not." He abruptly stood. "Haven't you been listening to me? My wife's situation could be dire. I must find her and the others."

Luna's stomach growled. She was hungry and tired. And she didn't have the energy to continue arguing with him. She had to get him to calm down. "Listen, no one's going to search in the dark, right?"

After a long hesitation, he loudly exhaled. "I suppose that's true."

"I promise you that if anyone washes up on the beach or is found in the water, I'll hear about it on Facebook in a New York minute. So there's nothing to do until morning. Why don't you come to my house and I'll fix us something to eat."

His expression relaxed. "I'm not sure what

you're referring to, but I must admit, I am in need of nourishment. I'll be no good to Evelyn in this state. If you're sure that we'll be told any news right away."

"I am." Thank heavens. "It's settled then."

They walked the rest of the way to Luna's cottage, with Colin remarking upon everything from the cars to the paved streets. He seemed genuinely completely unfamiliar with so much of the modern world.

Luna had never thought much before about time travel, but Colin was quickly making a believer of her. When they arrived at the cottage, she drew a relieved breath that her brother's car wasn't there.

Leo was forever giving her grief about the strays she always brought home—dogs, cats, even the occasional person. Lucky for her, she owned a business with a cat rescue in it, and she knew a couple of local dog rescues as well. As for her human strays, she had to work harder to find them homes, like the down-on-her-luck cocktail waitress from The Tiki Bar, who'd confided in Luna that her boyfriend had been hitting her. Luna had driven the young woman to a shelter in Daytona Beach. And then there was the runaway teenager who'd camped out for several days in the alley behind Cove Cat Café. Luna had let the girl sleep on her sofa for a week until a bed at a nearby runaway shelter became available.

But finding a place for an injured man who might be either delusional or a time traveler would be impossible. The notion of Colin being from another time seemed preposterous, yet so did a lot of things she'd seem in Cat's Paw Cove.

Luna unlocked the door and went in ahead of Colin. "Here we are."

When she switched on the overhead light, he gasped. "Forgive me," he said. "I am unused to such…wondrous feats."

Hecate, who was curled up on Luna's sofa, lifted her head for a moment then returned to her cat nap.

Luna hung her keys on the hook by the door and slung her shawl over the back of a chair. "I'll nuke something up for us to eat."

Colin gave her a blank stare. In the light, she was reminded just how handsome he was, even in his dirty, tattered clothes.

"I'll cook dinner," she clarified. "And I'll find dry clothes for you." Hurrying to the guest room, she grabbed a pair of Leo's jeans, a T-shirt, and some sneakers then returned to the living room.

Colin stood at her altar, his eyes wide. Pointing to the incense burner that was a statue of the maiden, mother, and crone, he shook his head then gestured toward the athame. "Are these tools of witchcraft?"

"They are. But don't worry. We don't sacrifice anything unless the moon is full."

He gasped.

"Kidding," she said.

Those mahogany eyes blazed. "Do you know what they do to witches where I come from?"

She remembered all too well the history of how witches were tortured and burned alive. Her mouth grew dry. Not that she feared he'd hurt her, she just hated for him to think badly of her. "Witches like me only try to do good in the world. We use herbs, oils, and crystals to bring about positive results."

"You mean like a magic spell?"

"Exactly." A little of the tension in her

shoulders eased, but Colin looked even warier. "Witchcraft has nothing to do with the devil or with hurting anyone. We're healers and teachers and nature lovers."

He backed away from the altar.

"Think of it this way," Luna continued. "A spell is merely a prayer with props."

Colin nodded thoughtfully. "I think I understand. You must be careful, though. If anyone sees these trinkets…."

"It's okay." She touched his arm and handed him Leo's clothes. "You're a little taller than my brother, but these should fit you. I'll wash the clothes you're wearing, although I can't promise you they'll survive the washing machine."

"Washing machine?" Colin shook his head, then unlaced his shirt and pulled it off.

Oh, my. She'd had no idea how muscular his shoulders were. She licked her lips. "Um, why don't you change in the bathroom. This way."

She led him down the hall and opened the door for him. "Would you like me to run you a bath?"

His gaze darted around the small room. "Aye, that would be good."

After she'd turned on the faucet and stopped the drain, she grabbed a towel from the shelf and set it on the sink. Standing so close to Colin, heat suffused her cheeks. Which was surely just the steam from the hot water. She shut off the faucet, cleared her throat, and backed toward the doorway. "Um…I'll be in the kitchen…if you need…anything."

Outside the room, she cringed. The man was even more unavailable than her past boyfriends had ever been—he was delusional at best, or a married man from the past.

Chapter Four

Colin dropped his shirt on the counter to his left and rolled his stiff, aching shoulders.

As he touched a large, purplish bruise on his side, his gaze shifted to his image reflected in a mirror that resembled a wood-framed window. This mirror wasn't warped or blotchy like the ones he'd used before.

He'd never seen such a clear reflection, except in still water. He could easily see the bluish shadows under his eyes, the dark stubble on his jaw and chin, as well as the sand clinging to his damp, stringy hair.

Was the crisp reflection also part of Luna's witchcraft?

Unease gripped him, even as her words echoed in his mind: *Witches like me only try to do good in the world.... We're healers and teachers and nature lovers.*

While his rational mind was still suspicious of her words, his heart believed she'd spoken the truth. Colin had learned to trust his instincts. They'd warned him, when he'd tried to negotiate with the men to whom his late father had owed money, that they intended to make him suffer for his parent's recklessness. They'd destroy him—not just take every last penny but besmirch his title as well, making it impossible for him to earn a living, get a loan, or make connections in society. All of England would shun him and his family, and he couldn't—*wouldn't*—allow his innocent wife and child to be caught up in such a situation.

His decision to flee the country had brought him not just to this strange land, but to Luna. Of all the folk he could have encountered on the beach tonight, he'd met her. He had to believe there was a reason why they'd been brought together. While he didn't understand the reason yet, his gut told him it was more than reuniting him with Evelyn. A matter to ponder further when he wasn't so bloody weary.

Colin stripped off his breeches and grimaced as sand showered onto the tile floor. Thankfully he had the clothes Luna had given him to wear—as long as he could figure out how to put them on.

He turned to the waiting pool of water. A bathtub, Luna had called it. It didn't look at all like the round tub made of wood in which he usually bathed. Nor had servants heated the water and hauled it to the room, a process that had usually taken a while. Steaming water had just poured out of the metal spigot, as if by magic.

More of Luna's witchcraft? No. More likely, servants were out of sight behind the tiled wall, heating the water and putting it through the spigot.

He leaned toward the wall and tapped on it with his knuckles. "Anyone there?"

No reply. He didn't hear any unusual sounds at all from behind the tiles.

Perhaps they'd heated as much water as they thought was necessary and had gone to attend to other duties. That must be it.

Determined to make the most of the bath before it got cold, he stepped into the tub and sat. Savoring the glorious warmth, he groaned and closed his eyes. How easily he could lean back and fall asleep, but he mustn't. Luna was waiting for him in the kitchen.

He picked up the oval-shaped soap nearby. It had a flowery fragrance that took his mind back to when he'd put his mouth close to Luna's ear to warn her of the pirates. He brought the soap close to his nose and inhaled deeply, vividly recalling the silky brush of her hair against his forearm and the protectiveness that had surged within him when he'd thought she was in danger.

Strong feelings, when he'd known her less than a day.

A grin tugged at his mouth. He remembered, too, how Luna's face had turned scarlet when he'd removed his shirt. She'd seemed nervous as well. Had she never seen a man's bare chest before?

Perhaps a man removing his shirt in front of a woman had significance in this land? For all he knew, it could be against the law. At some point, he should ask her about it; he didn't want to get her in trouble.

Colin lathered the soap. What a marvelous consistency—far gentler on the skin than what he was used to. Her soap made excellent bubbles, too. Fascinated, he lathered up a frothy handful then scrubbed himself from head to toe, washing away the sand and sea. He rubbed some in his dry hair too and leaned back to rinse it.

The water had turned a bit filmy, but he had yet to use what was in the bottle in the corner of the bathtub. Luna had called it poo. Something poo. An odd name, but she'd said it was to wash his hair. Since he was in the tub, he might as well. After finally getting the bottle open, he poured some of the glossy liquid into his hand then slapped it on the crown of his head.

Was that it?

He sat, water dripping from the ends of his hair. There had to be more to the process. He set his palm atop the poo and scrubbed. Ah, more bubbles! He used both hands and more poo until his whole head was one giant frothy mass. He submerged again and rinsed. He was liking this large bathtub more and more.

Sitting up, he swept water out of his eyes. How much better he felt than he had a short while ago.

Colin rose and reached for the towel Luna had left out for him. He had no doubt Evelyn would enjoy such a bathtub, too. He must look into getting one once they'd found a new home in Barbados.

Hearing the bathroom door open a few minutes later, Luna glanced down the hall and found Colin coming toward her with a towel around his waist. Before she could catch herself, she skimmed her gaze over his body. The fact that he had a killer body shouldn't matter to her, not one bit. Swallowing hard, she gestured toward her bedroom. "You can get dressed in there, first door on your right."

"Thank you." He headed to her room.

Luna's phone vibrated in her pocket. She took it out and found a text from Leo.

"Staying with Melissa tonight."

Who? Oh, his current girlfriend, Luna reminded herself. She texted back. *"Have fun."*

Seconds later, someone knocked at the front door. Hmm. It was late for anyone to stop by, and she had no clue how to explain Colin to anyone. But the visitor persisted, so Luna opened the door a crack and peeked outside.

Chuck stood there, holding a casserole dish. "I thought you'd be tired after the Founders' Day event. I'd have come earlier, only I ended up working late."

Heart pounding, she pasted on a smile. "That was very thoughtful, Chuck. I *am* tired. Exhausted, actually."

"Leo's not here, hmm?" He glanced past her then grinned at her. "So we're all alone."

Not really. And in truth, Luna had no desire to spend one-on-one time with Chuck, not yet. "Leo and whats-her-name made up." She feigned a yawn. "Yeah, I'm pretty wiped out."

He lifted the casserole higher. "You've got to eat. It's vegetarian. I found the recipe online."

Her stomach chose that moment to loudly growl. She resisted an eye roll. "Um, thanks. I'm not really up for company now, though."

As she opened the door wide enough to take the food, a loud crash exploded from the back of the house. She froze, gulped.

"Call the police, Luna." Chuck shoved the casserole at her and marched past her.

"No, stop!" When he did, she pursed her lips and huffed. "That was probably Hecate. She…got into a cabinet and clawed a bag of cat food. She's done that before. It's fine."

He folded his arms over his chest. "Hecate is

on the couch. What's going on, Luna?"

She could hardly tell him that she had another guy in her bedroom. Not that she and Chuck were even dating, although he'd made his interest plain. "I...I brought another stray home." Not a lie, really.

"Another cat?"

She set down the casserole and shrugged. "I'll take him to the café tomorrow."

Chuck huffed. "Okay. I'll leave. If you're sure you're all right."

"I'll be fine." She patted his arm. "Thanks, Chuck."

The second he left, she rushed down the hall and knocked on her bedroom door.

Colin muttered a curse.

She went in. Her television, casting its indigo light in the room, was on the floor. "What happened?"

Colin looked even more handsome in Leo's clothes. "I don't understand things here. When I sat on the bed, this box fell." He showed her the TV remote. "I accidentally stepped on it, and that window lit up like ten candles. And there was a ship in the window." He scratched his head. "Which wasn't a window at all."

Luna took a better look at the TV screen. A scene from Moby Dick was frozen there—Gregory Peck's Captain Ahab on the deck of his ship. She picked up the television and returned it to the dresser. "You're right. It isn't a window. It's...." How could she explain television to him? "It's more like a painting that comes to life."

"But how? I don't understand." Colin squeezed his eyes shut then sheepishly lifted the T-shirt a few inches to show her the open fly of his jeans. "And I don't know how to fasten these breeches."

"I promise I'll be gentle." Face heating, she moved closer and showed him how the zipper worked.

"Thank you," he said. "I might need your help with that again."

Luna grinned. "Is that right?"

Colin shrugged. "I suppose I could do it from now on."

She held back a smile.

Their gazes met and held. A zing of heat ricocheted between them. Mouth dry as dust, she backed away and cleared her throat. "Let's eat. We need to talk, Colin."

At the small table in the dining area, Colin practically inhaled the macaroni and cheese casserole while Luna picked at hers. She researched the early history of Cat's Paw Cove on her phone, so she would be sure of her facts. "So your wife's name is Evelyn Wilshire?"

"Aye. Evelyn Grisham Wilshire." He shoveled another bite of pasta into his mouth and groaned with pleasure.

"You remember what we discussed earlier, right? That hundreds of years have passed since that shipwreck you spoke about."

He stopped eating and frowned. "Aye. But it's so difficult to fathom."

"It sure is." Mating her fingers, she explained what she knew about the original settlers of the town. "Somehow, you've traveled to the twenty-first century. This is America—Cat's Paw Cove, Florida, to be exact. I have no clue how you happened to get here, but this town is quite a magical place. Anything's possible."

"But how…I don't…Evelyn, our child. What happened to them?"

Her heart ached for him. "Most of the passengers survived the wreck then settled here, eventually establishing this town. We can head over to the Shipwreck Museum in the morning. Maybe you'll find more answers to your questions there."

Colin buried his head in his hands, and said nothing for several minutes.

Luna cleared away their plates to give him time to absorb what she'd told him. When she returned a few minutes later, he was sitting on the sofa petting Hecate.

"There were cats on the ship with us," he said.

"I've heard that. Hecate is descended from those original Sherwood cats."

"Really?"

She nodded but decided not to mention that most Sherwood cats possessed a magical gift of some sort. Why lay even more on poor Colin. Besides, Luna hadn't yet discovered if Hecate had a magical side.

Colin leaned his head back on the cushions. Luna went to fetch him a glass of water, and some wine for herself. When she returned, Colin was fast asleep.

She picked up the afghan from the rocking chair and draped it over him then turned out the lights.

What in the world was she going to do with him?

Colin woke to a soft tap on his cheek. His eyes still shut, he sighed and waved his hand to shoo away the moth that had brushed his skin. The pests had stowed away in his and Evelyn's clothes, but they'd find a way to get rid of them once they reached Barbados.

Savoring the quietness of the ship's cabin, he listened for the creaks and groans of the vessel that had become familiar to him, as well as the shouts of the crew on deck. The sea must be calm today.

He snuggled deeper into the pillow beneath his head. There was no rush for him to get up. Evelyn must still be asleep, and he didn't want to wake her—

Tap.

Tap-tap.

A persistent moth...or it wasn't a moth at all.

Turning his face, he cracked his eyelids open, just in time to see a cat rise up and bat his face with a front paw.

Hecate.

All that had happened the previous day rushed into Colin's mind. He abruptly sat up, wincing at the pains in his body, to find he was still on the couch in Luna's living room. Beyond the coverings over the nearby window—Luna had called them blinds—it was still dark outside, but he heard the sound of drawers opening and closing from her bedroom.

With a playful *brrtt*, the feline darted backward, spun, and raced off down the hallway.

At least someone was in high spirits this morning.

Colin leaned forward, set his elbows on his knees, and plowed his hands into his hair. Luna had spread a curious-looking blanket over him while he'd slept and the top half of it was now puddled in his lap.

It isn't 1645 anymore.

More than three hundred seventy years have passed since then.

His eyes stung as he remembered Luna's words. His former life was gone. All that he'd known just yesterday had been gone for hundreds of years. It seemed impossible. But it wasn't.

What was he going to do? He didn't have any money, didn't know anyone apart from Luna. He didn't understand how a small box could turn a TV on and off. Luna had called it modern teknolagee, whatever that was.

The enormity of his situation threatened to drown him, but he focused on regaining control of his emotions. He hadn't explored all of his options yet. Luna had told him Cat's Paw Cove was a magical place and that anything was possible. Perhaps there was a way for him to go back to his own time. Maybe Luna would use her witchcraft to send him home; a somewhat unsettling thought, but she'd been kinder to him than folk in his own time, and so, he'd continue to place his trust in her.

He heard muffled footsteps. As he raised his head, Luna appeared, dressed in garments similar to what she'd worn yesterday. As Hecate bounded past her into the kitchen, Luna smiled at him. "'Morning."

"Good morning," he said, determined she wouldn't see any trace of tears in his eyes.

"I'm glad you're awake. I know it's a very early start, but I have to get to the bakery. It's probably best if you come with me."

If she thought it best, he would go. "All right."

"How did you sleep?"

"Very well. You?"

"Fine." She wrinkled her nose. "Except when Hecate was snoring."

Colin laughed in surprise. "Your cat snores?"

"Apparently, so." Luna switched on the lights in the kitchen and opened a cupboard. "Do you like to start the day with coffee? Or, since you're British, do you prefer tea?"

"I don't believe I've ever had coffee."

"We do serve it at the café, but I can't wake up unless I have some first thing." Luna ran water into an oddly-shaped glass vessel. He made a mental note to ask her later about the hot water and her household servants. "I just bought an organic blend," she continued. "I'll make it and you can see how you like it."

He managed a grin. "I will try most things once."

"Good to know." After pouring the water into some kind of machine on her counter, she pushed a button and turned back to him. "We should check your head wound and change the bandage."

"It feels fine—"

"Don't be stubborn."

His brows rose. "It's my wound."

"Yeah, but we don't want it to become infected."

He'd seen corrupted wounds. He'd known men who'd had limbs sawn off because of infection. "Do what you will, then."

"Do what I will?" Luna whistled. "You might finally be starting to trust me."

"I might—" He paused and inhaled deeply. "What is that marvelous smell?"

"Coffee."

He had to taste this coffee. He headed for the gurgling machine.

Luna caught his arm, stopping him. "It hasn't

finished brewing. Once I've finished tending your wound, it should be done."

His attention shifted from her slender hand gripping his arm. Slowly, his gaze slid along her arm, up over her shoulder, to her face. He swallowed hard, for he couldn't explain the feelings stirred up by her touch. Was she using her magic on him?

Averting her gaze, she gestured to a chair at the kitchen table. "Why don't you sit there? I'll get the supplies."

He sat, the chair squeaking as it took his weight. Luna returned to the kitchen, went to a different cupboard and came back with gauze, a tube of ointment, and several other items. She put them on the table beside him. "I'll try not to hurt you."

Her voice had wobbled a bit. Was she worried about her skill in treating him, or was she unsettled about being so close to him? Trying to ease the situation, he said: "At least you are not using things like those at the medic station."

"Only because I don't own any."

He cast her a narrowed glance. "If that was meant to reassure me—"

Chuckling, she moved closer. Her leg pressed against his thigh as her fingers began pulling away his bandage. "I'll make this quick."

He'd heard what she'd said, but his mind wasn't on the conversation. He could hardly think at all, with the heat of her body touching his, her flowery scent teasing him, and hunger for her kindling in his veins.

He laced his hands together, resisting the urge to slide his arm around her and pull her into his lap. He was a married man; a husband and soon to be a father.

He shouldn't desire anyone but his wife.

"Your wound's got a lot of bruising around it, but I expect that's part of the healing process." Luna poured liquid from a bottle and gently swabbed his injury then opened a tube of ointment. Her fingertips glided over his forehead.

A hot shiver raced through him.

She immediately stilled. "Did I hurt you?"

"No," he ground out. He wouldn't describe what he was feeling as pain.

"Colin—"

"Are you almost finished?" He hadn't meant to be brusque, but her ministrations really were a form of torture. "I think I need coffee."

"I know I do." Paper crinkled as she opened clean bandages and applied them. "There, all done." She gathered up the supplies and stepped away, breaking contact. "We'll put our coffee in tumblers with lids. That way we can drink it on the way to the café."

Chapter Five

On the way to the café, Colin scratched his head. "Where are the horses pulling this wagon?"

"There's a motor under the hood," Luna supplied.

"Are they miniature horses?" He searched under the dashboard.

"No, it's…." She sighed. "More than a hundred years ago, an inventor made the first car…er…horseless carriage."

"How does it work?"

She parked behind Cove Cat Café and shut off the engine. "Honestly, I have no idea." But she had a plan to get him a bit more up to speed about modern conveniences, which would keep him occupied as well.

Inside the café, she brought Colin into the cat room and set him up in a comfortable seat with her laptop and a latte. She opened a website that listed every major invention in the past century then showed him how to scroll through the page.

"I'll bring you a cinnamon bun as soon as they're done," she told him. Then she headed to the kitchen to start baking, checking on him every few minutes.

He seemed fascinated by what he read. Trying to imagine how out of sorts he must feel, Luna's gut twisted. Not only had he lost everything and everyone he'd known, but now he was in a world completely foreign to him.

When several types of her pastries came out of the oven, she put one of each on a plate and headed to give the confections to Colin. She stopped at the window that separated the café from the cat room.

Colin was down on the floor, playing with the grey tabby and the Siamese mix. One of the tuxedo kittens was on his shoulder, nibbling on Colin's ear. Another kitten crawled up his chest to settle in the crook of his arm. He cradled the little ball of fluff so tenderly, smiling down at it, saying something Luna couldn't hear.

Her stomach fluttered. Getting too attached to Colin was a terrible idea, though. She had to think of him as yet another stray for which she would find a more permanent solution. After grabbing a few napkins, she pushed through the glass door. "Hungry?"

"Quite." Gently moving the kitties off of him, he stood and joined her on a sofa.

"We don't normally allow food in this part of the café, but I happen to be close with the owner." She set the food down on the coffee table, then handed him a wet wipe from the box.

He just stared at the wipe, so she took it from him and cleaned his hands with it.

Colin bit into the raspberry cheesecake bar and moaned. "The food in this world is like heaven."

"Didn't they have good desserts in England?"

Luna tore off a piece of a cinnamon bun for herself.

"Not like these. We used to have preserved fruits, wafers, and jelly when times were good." His features clouded for a moment. "There wasn't always money for sugar."

"That's a great reason to stay in the twenty-first century," she joked.

Colin stiffened. "I've been reading about the many wondrous innovations you have here. One thing I can't do here, though, is meet my son or daughter, or be a husband to Evelyn."

Before Luna could apologize for her insensitivity, the door to the cat room opened.

Her brother stopped in his tracks and looked from Colin to her. "Good morning." Closing the distance to the couch, he offered Colin his hand. "Hey, I'm Leo."

Colin shook with him. "Colin Wilshire."

Leo slowly nodded. "Nice to meet you. I thought I knew every Wilshire in town. I guess you guys are crawling out of the woodwork, hmm?" He trailed his gaze over Colin. "Dude, are you wearing my clothes?"

Colin stood up and puffed out his chest.

Before Colin could say anything, Luna inserted herself between the men. Centering a hand on her brother's chest, she eased him back. "I can explain. Colin's clothes were in bad shape."

Leo shrugged. "And?"

"And I borrowed some that you'd left at my house."

He pulled Luna aside. "You two were looking pretty cozy when I came in. And now he's glaring at me as if he's a jealous lover or something. I thought you and Chuck were…you know."

She glanced over her shoulder at Colin. Sure enough, jealousy was exactly what she saw in his blazing eyes. Or maybe it was just protectiveness. Either way, she was flattered. There was that fluttery feeling again. "Chuck and I are just friends," she told Leo. "Colin had nowhere to go. He doesn't know anyone here."

"Okay, cool." He held up his hands in surrender. "None of my business. But if he's a Wilshire, he must have family in town."

Her brother would think she was crazy if she tried to explain that Colin might be a time traveler. "He's…estranged from them."

Leo nodded his understanding. To Colin, he said, "It's all good, bro. Keep the threads."

"Thanks," Luna said. "I've got to take Colin…on an errand. All the baking is done. I just need to finish frosting the rest of the cinnamon buns. Jordan should be here any minute. Would you mind if I left for a while?"

With another glance at Colin, Leo shrugged. "Not a problem. Just be careful, okay?"

"I promise." After Leo left the room, she returned to Colin. "Give me ten minutes, and then we can head over to the museum, okay?"

"That's fine." Picking up another pastry, he said, "It will take me that long to finish eating these."

Colin studied the rectangular yellow bar with a dusting of white powder. He should probably stop eating, but he was ravenous this morning, and Luna was an excellent baker.

Careful not to get white powder all over her laptop, he bit into the bar. Tangy lemon and a sugary sweetness filled his mouth.

"Mmm." As the sound rumbled in his throat, he closed his eyes, savoring the perfect blend of flavors. His thoughts slipped back to the grand feasts his parents had held when he was a boy. How vividly he could still see the gleaming silver, the sparkling crystal, and the sumptuous cakes, some decorated with violets, roses, and curls of lemon rind. His mother, who'd died just after his tenth birthday, had still been alive then to fuss over the table decorations and tell him to go run a comb through his messy hair.

A wry smile tugged at his mouth. How curious that of the few things he remembered about his mother, he recalled her ordering him about, trying to make him presentable for their guests. So much pretense. That desire to live richly, to be included in the right social circles, had gotten his father into debt that he'd foolishly chosen to ignore.

Colin washed down the mouthful of lemon bar with a sip of latte. He could either let the fact that he'd been brought to another time destroy him, or he could use his wits to try and get back to 1645. His father might have allowed his circumstances to ruin him, used them as an excuse to neglect his responsibilities, but Colin wasn't going to do the same. His inventions—and the ones he was reading about now—showed the ingenuity of the human mind. He wasn't going to stop trying to get back to Evelyn until he'd exhausted ideas, although part of him would sorely regret having to say goodbye to Luna.

He finished the lemon bar and washed his hands with another wet wipe. He had to say, he approved of the wipes: a pleasant convenience that meant he could clean his hands—or any part of him, really—anytime and anywhere.

Colin focused on what was on the laptop screen. As he began reading about the steam engine, anticipation tingled within him. He'd experienced the same thrilling feeling when he'd worked on his own designs, especially his two-wheeled contraption. He'd written of his excitement, of his hopes for building a sample of what he'd drawn, in several letters to Matthew.

Did Luna feel such excitement when she invented a new recipe? He glanced through the window that divided the cat room from the café but couldn't see her. He could easily imagine her, though, busy in the kitchen, her hair covered by a mesh cap that looked both ridiculous and charming. The first time he'd seen her wearing it, he'd wanted to walk over to her and pull it off, but there was obviously a reason why she wore one. Maybe it was to discourage potential suitors from courting her while she concentrated on her baking. That made perfect sense, for she wouldn't want to be distracted and thus cause her confections to burn.

Colin scrolled a little further, scratching his chin as he read. The fellow in the picture accompanying the information on steam engines looked a bit like Leo. While at first Colin had resented her obvious affection for Leo, he'd been relieved to find out the man was her brother. It was good Luna had family close by, to know she had someone in her life she could depend on.

Colin's thoughts drifted back to the storm-ravaged sea, to the last time he'd seen Evelyn. He prayed she and the babe were all right. What about the young Bell girl and the other passengers?

Perhaps he could use the laptop to find out. It seemed to hold the kind of information one would normally glean from books. It might even be able to tell him how to travel through time.

A renewed excitement welled within him. When he found a good opportunity, he'd ask Luna how to do a search of the laptop's knowledge. For now, he'd indulge his inventor's soul, keep scrolling, and commit to memory as much as he could.

Luna completed her kitchen work, then went to get Colin from the cat room. He was hunched over her laptop, totally engrossed in his reading while holding two cats, and absently dangling a toy for a third.

Was he always this adorable? No, she absolutely refused to acknowledge how sweet she found him. Steeling herself, she took her car keys out of her purse. "The museum should be open by now. Are you ready to go?"

He smiled up at her. "Quite. Thank you for letting me read this…whatever it is."

"It's called a webpage."

Setting the kittens aside, he got up and handed her the empty plate that had held at least three thousand calories worth of confections. "And thank you for the sweets."

As they left, she dropped the plate in the sink. Morning sun lit up the streets as the town came to life. Turning onto Sherwood Boulevard, Luna stopped short to avoid hitting a young woman on a bike who'd ridden right through the red light.

The woman waved apologetically before continuing through the intersection.

Colin gasped. "What was that?"

Following his gaze to the biker, Luna said, "A bicycle. I guess they didn't have those in your time, hmm?"

He gripped the dashboard. "No, but I was working on that very idea."

"What do you mean?"

"I used to tinker with new ideas; inventions, I suppose. I'd planned to continue my work in Barbados, even make a living at it."

Sirens interrupted their conversation. When Luna noticed flashing lights in her rearview mirror, she pulled to the side of the road. A police car rushed past her toward the beach.

"What a terrible noise," Colin remarked.

That was the sheriff or a deputy. "I hope everything's all right."

Minutes later, when they reached the boardwalk, she realized that something was going on. Two patrol cars were parked near the entrance to the Shipwreck Museum. She recognized the taller man as Sheriff Higgins. "Uh, oh."

"What is it?" Colin asked.

She parked her car and waited as the other officer roped off the walkway that led to the museum. "Something must have happened at the museum." Luna's intuition turned on like a supernatural light switch. Colin could be in danger here. Or was she just picking up on centuries-old energy from the raised ship? After all, people had perished on the Guinevere.

Shielding his eyes, Collin leaned closer to the window. "The sails are different, but that's the Guinevere I sailed on. I'm sure of it. I have to see it."

Before she could stop him, Colin jumped out of the car and raced toward the boat.

Luna went after him. As she ran, she said the words in her head to place a protection spell around Colin, just in case.

Oh, great Goddess, I summon thee to protect Colin from any and all dangers. So mote it be.

A deputy held up his hand, warning Colin to stop. "This a crime scene, sir. You can't go any farther."

Fists clenched at his sides, Colin persisted. "I must board my ship."

"*Your* ship?"

Luna got there and hooked Colin's arm, easing him back. "Let's find out what's going on, okay? We'll see the Guinevere, just not right now."

Colin struggled for patience.

Now that he was so close to the ship, to reconnecting with his past life, he wanted to get back on the boat right away.

The familiar surroundings might spark memories he'd forgotten. They might even inspire ideas to help him to return to his own century. The need became a raw ache in his chest.

"Colin," Luna murmured.

"I don't want to wait."

"I understand—"

"You can't possibly understand." He hadn't meant to snap at her, but the words were filled with frustration and disappointment.

"Hey," she said, touching his face.

The caress only deepened his pain. He wrenched away.

Anguish registered in Luna's gaze. It hurt him to know he'd hurt her.

Colin dragged in several breaths, trying to rein in his turmoil. He must be careful. The official who'd barred his way moments ago was still watching him.

"We will go on board at a better time," Luna soothed.

Colin's head began to pound; he reached up, his fingers skating over the bandage. "When will that be? Later today? Days from now?"

"Well, we'll need to find out when the museum will reopen."

"How can we find that out?"

Luna pushed aside strands of hair the sea breeze had just blown across her cheek. "The Historical Society runs the museum. We can check their webpage for an update."

"This society," he said. "Would they know what happened to the people I was traveling with on the ship?"

"They might."

Ah. Some good news.

"They would also know if things…were found on the vessel?"

"What kind of things?"

He shrugged, reluctant to discuss his drawings with her just yet. "Items that belonged to passengers."

"I did hear that the society has some artifacts from the Guinevere in their collection. I expect those will be on display. To be honest, though, the Guinevere's restoration team didn't release much information to the general public. It was all kept very secret."

While traveling on the ship, Colin hadn't become aware of any reason that would have warranted a need for secrecy. Had the pirates that had lurked on the horizon before the storm somehow known of the secret? Had the captain and crew been paid to deliver riches to Barbados, but not told the others on the vessel? "Did the restorers explain their reasons for the secrecy?" he asked.

"No. I heard through the grapevine, though, that they expected to find treasure."

Luna listened to grapevines? He hadn't realized they talked; he'd thought they just grew grapes. "The riches were concealed on the ship?"

Luna nodded.

"Gold? Jewels?"

"No one really knows. Even the site in Florida where the boat was being restored was kept secret. The specialists didn't want people breaking in, using metal detectors, or prying up floorboards and causing more damage to the vessel."

Had the restorers discovered the wooden tube Colin had hidden in the cabin ? It seemed the only explanation for what he'd seen a short while ago: a bicycle.

Knowing that his idea had been viable left him in awe. But, his sense of wonder was tainted by the knowledge someone had taken his invention, claimed it as his own, and profited from it.

That invention was to have supported Colin's family.

He had to know if his sketches were still where he'd left them, as soon as possible.

How, though, did he get past the two burly officials who were now eyeing him as though he was under suspicion?

Sheriff Higgins came over. "Who's your friend, Luna?"

She gulped. "G'morning, RJ. This is Colin. He's…a history buff. He was so looking forward to exploring the ship."

The sheriff leveled a wary gaze at Colin before returning his attention to Luna. "A history buff."

She nodded.

"Someone broke into the museum earlier this morning." Narrowing his eyes at Colin, he folded his arms over his broad chest. "You know anything about that, Colin?"

"I know that I need to get on the ship. You have to let me through."

RJ stood taller. "No, I don't."

Luna shored up the protective energy she'd raised around Colin. "He's just…traveled a long way for this. Any idea when it will reopen?"

"After we finish our investigation," RJ replied. "Which we'll do as fast as we can."

"Thanks, I understand." She waved to the

sheriff then pulled Colin away. "I'm as frustrated as you are, but this is out of our control." Although part of her was a tiny bit relieved. What if Colin found out that his wife had also time traveled? Or if he found some way to return to his time on the vessel? Despite only knowing him for one day, she'd already grown to like him. She had no right to her feelings. He belonged to Evelyn, and to the seventeenth century.

Colin gritted his teeth. "I need answers."

"I know." She took his hand. "And I promise that I'll help you find them. Let's go back to my place for a little while. Hopefully, they'll be able to reopen the museum soon."

After several beats, he finally acquiesced. "Fine."

A few minutes later, she parked her car at her house. Colin hadn't said a word during the short drive, but his irritation was clear.

Inside the cottage, Luna powered up her laptop and opened the same website Colin had found so fascinating earlier. "I'm going to bake something."

"I thought you'd finished your work."

"I did." She sighed. "Since I was a kid, baking has always been sort of an outlet for me. I pour everything into it—stress, anger, you name it."

His expression softened. "Did you have a difficult childhood?"

Her insides knotted with a familiar pain. "It could have been worse, but I wish it had been better."

Colin motioned for her to join him on the sofa.

She sat down and grinned at him. "Are you my shrink now?"

He furrowed his brow. "Are there people who can shrink others now?"

Laughing, she shook her head. "It's an expression."

"Tell me why you needed an outlet for your feelings when you were a child."

"We just moved around a lot. Mom was a lot like my brother is now. She went from lover to lover, always putting them before Leo and me. I guess that's why he is the way he is."

"I'm sorry." Colin draped his arm over her shoulder. "It's good that you had your brother, though."

"That's true." It was nice having Colin comfort her. For longer than she cared to admit, Hecate had been her only confidante.

Luna glanced around the room for the cat. Hmm. Hecate spent every morning in the living room, curled up in the sliver of morning sunlight on the window seat. The hair on the back of Luna's neck stood on end. She got up and started searching for the cat. "Hecate? Hecate? Here, kitty, kitty."

"What's wrong?" Colin followed her into the kitchen.

"I can't find her."

"I'm sure she's here somewhere." He opened each cabinet and looked inside.

Luna's fear ramped up. Her temples throbbed. "She always comes when I call her."

But after a thorough search of the cottage and yard, Hecate still hadn't turned up. Tears stung Luna's eyes. She went into the bathroom to grab a tissue and froze at the sight of the open window. "Oh, no!"

Colin was there in an instant. "What?"

She pointed to the window.

"Oh, God," he said. "I opened it last night after

my bath. I must have forgotten to shut it. I'm so sorry, Luna."

A sob rose in her throat.

Colin grasped Luna's shoulders. "We'll find her, I promise." He pulled her into his arms and pressed a gentle kiss to the top of her head.

His embrace felt way better than it should—as if she was where she'd always belonged. But now wasn't the time to indulge in useless fantasies. Hecate was missing, and Luna had to bring her home.

Colin held her at arms' length. "Can you do a spell to bring her back?"

"Good idea. I can try." Why hadn't she thought of that? She backed out of Colin's arms and felt suddenly colder for the loss of contact. "Would you bring me Hecate's food bowl from the kitchen?"

Colin nodded and left the room.

Luna had never done a spell in the presence of one of the town's regular folks, or 'Regs' as the local Magicals called them. But she'd already told Colin what she was, so she opened the drawer under her altar and took out a green candle and her Book of Shadows, where she wrote down all of her spells. Then she grabbed Hecate's favorite toy mouse from the basket next to the sofa.

When Colin returned with Hecate's bowl, she took it from him. "If you'd rather leave while I do this, I'll understand."

He hesitated only a second before shaking his head. "I want to be here for you. And for Hecate."

Although he didn't touch her, Luna felt him wrap her in comfort. "Thank you," she whispered. Then she set the green candle inside Hecate's bowl and lit it. Drawing a deep breath, she closed her eyes and called up an image of her cat. "Oh, great goddess, I call upon you. My little Hecate has gone astray. I wish for her return today. Keep her safe from harm, and return her now back to my arms."

Opening her eyes, she stared at the candle. "Please, goddess, bring back my Hecate." Luna concentrated all her magical energy on her kitty.

A knock on the door startled her.

"Shall I?" Colin asked.

Holding her breath, Luna nodded.

Colin opened the door, and Fiona Bell stood there holding Hecate.

"Hi," Fiona said. "Is Luna here?"

Relief rushed through Luna as she brushed past Colin. "You found her!"

Fiona handed the cat to Luna. "I was walking on the beach, foraging for beautyberry and seagrape when I saw her walking toward me."

Luna snuggled Hecate's white fur and breathed in the smell of the beach. "You had me so worried," she told the cat.

"I didn't realize that she was yours," the blond said. "So I took her to the café. I figured Jordan would know if she was a stray or if she belonged to someone in town."

Luna gave Fiona a one-armed hug. "I can't thank you enough."

"Jordan immediately recognized her, of course," Fiona said. "Oh, and Jordan told me to tell you that she knows Hecate's magical power now. I guess they had a conversation." Fiona glanced at Colin. "I'm sorry, we haven't met, have we?" She offered her hand. "Fiona Bell."

Colin shook her hand. "Colin Wilshire."

"Wilshire?" Fiona lifted an eyebrow then met Luna's stare.

Luna nodded, but she wanted to hear about Hecate's magical gift. "What did Jordan say?"

Fiona took a few steps closer and lowered her voice. "Can I say it in front of…?" She tipped her chin toward Colin.

"Go ahead," Luna said.

"Well," Fiona started, "your cat—being a Sherwood—has the gift of being able to find portals to other times. She was heading to the Shipwreck Museum when I found her, although Jordan couldn't get Hecate to explain why."

Colin's jaw dropped.

Luna gulped. Was her kitty's power the reason that a sexy time traveler had walked into Luna's life? If so, Hecate had the power to send Colin back to the seventeenth century.

Chapter Six

ecate could find portals to other times.

He could return to 1645. To Evelyn.

Colin's throat tightened as he met Luna's gaze. Her shocked expression revealed she'd had no idea of her feline's special ability. His gut instincts told him she wasn't acting right now; that if she'd known before of a way to send him back to his own century, so that he'd find happiness, she would have told him about it. Her generous heart wouldn't have let her keep such a secret.

He could only imagine the emotions Luna was experiencing, and what the cat's ability might mean for a witch who wanted to help other lost souls in Cat's Paw Cove. He doubted her shock related to him being able to go home. They'd only known each other for such a short while; she'd most likely be relieved to be rid of him, a burden who depended on her for so many things.

As though sensing his thoughts, Luna looked back at Fiona. "I can't say how much it means to have Hecate home. Thank you."

"Happy to help." Fiona's intrigued gaze shifted back to Colin. "So, did you come to town for the reception?"

"Reception?" he asked

"Yeah. The special event the Historical Society put on a few days ago."

Judging by her puzzled gaze, Luna didn't know what Fiona was talking about, either.

"Unfortunately, I missed it," Colin said.

"Now that you mention it, I do vaguely remember something about a reception." Luna set struggling Hecate down. "I was so busy prepping for yesterday's celebrations, though, I didn't keep track."

"It was by invitation only," Fiona said. "The society volunteers tracked down as many relatives of the original Founding Families as they could and invited them to preview the museum before it opened to the public."

"A nice idea," Colin said.

"Very nice. Some of the guests wore historical clothing. Some even flew all the way from Europe to attend." Fiona sighed. "There were several Wilshires there that night. I would have thought you'd have been invited, Colin, since you're a Wilshire and also named after one of the original passengers."

If only she knew he *was* one of the original passengers. Fighting a smile, he said, "I must have missed the invitation."

"With luck, there will be another reception sometime. Maybe when they find the treasure that's rumored to be on the Guinevere, right?"

He managed a laugh. "Right."

"I'd better be on my way." Fiona glanced down the driveway to the street. "I need to get back to my foraging. Hopefully the police will be finished at the museum."

"Did you hear any news of the investigation?" Luna asked.

"Only that someone broke in. Minor damage, thankfully. RJ did tell me nothing was stolen, which seems kind of weird. I mean, why break in and not take anything?"

"That does seem odd," Luna murmured, glancing at Colin.

"Any idea what was damaged?" he asked.

"RJ didn't say, but I'm sure the *Cat's Paw Cove Courier* will have an update in tomorrow's paper." Fiona stepped backward and waved. "Gotta run. I'll come visit you at the café soon, Luna."

Colin waited until Fiona had reached the sidewalk, where the sounds of a neighbor mowing his lawn and cars driving by would muffle his and Luna's conversation. "I *have* to get on the ship."

Luna closed the front door and folded her arms. "You can't. Not when there's an active investigation."

His mind raced. He mustn't be reckless, especially when he didn't know the laws of this time. If the police found out about his debts in 1645, would they arrest and jail him? He'd never get back to Evelyn then. "I wonder…. Do you know anyone in the Historical Society?"

She gnawed her bottom lip. "I do. Some of the ladies visit the café."

"Could you contact them? Tell them that regrettably, I missed the reception but would love a private viewing of the museum?"

"I can try."

He touched her arm. "Thanks."

His touch obviously affected her because she

drew in a breath and pushed back her shoulders. "The woman I'm going to try first loves cinnamon buns. I'll sweeten the deal by offering her a few boxes. I'll make sure it's okay for me to bring Hecate, too."

His heart constricted. Luna expected that once they got to the ship, and the cat located a portal, Colin would be going through. They might never see each other again.

What he would give to have different choices before him. But, he couldn't abandon Evelyn. He had to believe she and their child survived the storm, and that she would be trying to find him. He couldn't bear to think of her pregnant, alone, and likely injured. She might have lost the few possessions they'd taken on the ship, which left her vulnerable in ways he couldn't bear to contemplate. He'd vowed on their wedding day to be faithful to her; to love, care for, and protect her; and that's what he must do.

Still, he couldn't deny he cared for Luna, too. His eyes burned as he released her arm. "Having tasted your baking, I'm sure the woman won't be able to say no."

Luna nodded and walked away. Colin went to the living room and sat, waiting, stroking Hecate who'd jumped up beside him on the sofa. A moment later, he heard Luna talking. She must be using the device she'd called a cell phone.

She returned and smiled at him. "It's all set."

He quickly rose. "Really?"

"The police should be finished at the museum by two o'clock. It will remain closed until tomorrow, but my friend Roberta will meet us there and let us in."

Anticipation and regret tangled within him.

"She said she couldn't resist, what with you

being a Wilshire and the cinnamon bun bribe."

He chuckled. "I will be sure to thank her myself."

Time seemed to crawl by as they waited until ten-to-two, the time Luna had said they'd leave the house. They'd agreed it would be better for Colin to be wearing the garments he'd had on when she'd found him on the beach, not Leo's T-shirt and jeans.

At some point over the past day, she'd washed Colin's clothes. He hadn't seen her scrub and rinse the garments, but somehow, she had—and very thoroughly, too.

"How did you get my shirt so white?" Colin had never seen it so clean. He brought it to his nose and inhaled the crisp, fresh scent and wished everything he wore could smell that good.

"My washing machine's fairly new, and I threw in some vinegar and borax."

Washing machine? Borax? He thought to ask, but was there really any point? He'd soon be hundreds of years in the past again.

He sat beside her, his arm behind her along the back of the sofa, while she mended the tears in his clothes. He'd told her not to bother, but she'd insisted, perhaps to keep herself busy while they waited. Her blue hair gleamed in the sunlight from the nearby window, some strands tumbling forward over her shoulder.

He yearned to brush those strands out of the way for her. He longed to sink his fingers into her tresses and tilt her face toward him so he could kiss her. He ached to taste her lips, slowly and deeply, so he could remember that treasured kiss for the rest of his living days. But, he didn't dare.

"There." She set the needle in a pincushion and shook out his breeches. "Not the greatest sewing job, but it will do."

"You're very kind to have bothered."

She cast him a sidelong glance. "I'm sure you'd like to be presentable when you meet Evelyn again."

"It will be odd to be back in 1645, when I have experienced the wonders of your world." He finally gave in to the need to touch her hair. "No poo—"

"Shampoo," she corrected with a grin.

"Right. No webpages, either. No cars. No lemon bars."

She patted his knee. "If all goes well, you'll get to see your baby right after it's born. See his or her face for the first time."

"Yes," he whispered. He did want that. Very much.

Luna busied herself in the kitchen to keep her mind off of what would happen in just a couple of hours—Colin would likely disappear from her life. Pulling a bunch of dry ingredients out of the cabinet, she ticked off ideas for new cupcakes. "Maybe I'll try a maple-bourbon cupcake, or a rhubarb and raspberry one."

Colin sat at the breakfast bar. "Both sound delicious."

She turned her back to him as she set up her mixer. Better not to look at him right now. In time, she hoped to forget that handsome face—that strong jaw, and those amazing brown eyes.

"I'm sorry if I've hurt you," he said.

Tears stung her eyes, but she refused to let him see. Making Colin feel guilty for wanting to go back where he'd come from would be selfish of her. "You haven't done anything wrong." She whisked flour, sugar, salt and baking powder in a large metal bowl.

He came into the kitchen and lifted her chin, so she was forced to look up at him. "That doesn't mean either of us will walk away from this unscathed, though."

Luna clenched her jaw to keep her emotions in check. "Our feelings pale compared to your child's needs. And your wife's. I grew up without a father, and I'd never inflict that upon anyone, not if there's a way to avoid it."

"How did you lose your father?"

"He left us when Leo and I were just toddlers." She winced at the painful memories. "Another woman was involved."

"Your father was a scoundrel then."

She couldn't help her smirk. "Definitely."

"Mine wasn't much better," he said. "Gambling was his undoing. After his death, I was saddled with his debts. My father's debtors refused to even negotiate with me. Had I stayed, they'd have ruined me, and I wouldn't have been able to support my family. I had no choice but to leave England."

A lump lodged in the back of her throat. "That's awful. I'm sorry."

Colin shrugged off her sympathy. "It's all in the past."

She had to smile at the irony of his statement. "You can say that again."

Their gazes locked, and they both laughed,

which lightened the moment.

Colin took her hands. "Somehow, in just a few days, I've grown to care about you, Luna. If my situation were different, I'd stay."

Nope, she refused to give voice to her feelings. She couldn't be falling for him. Heck, he didn't even really exist in the twenty-first century. Twisting away from him, she went back to her mixing bowl.

"I feel like an awful wretch for dragging you into my…mess."

She hated for him to blame himself for fate's folly. "You didn't ask to be thrust into the future, ripped out of your own time."

"If it wasn't for my responsibilities there…." He exhaled loudly. "Staying here is quite tempting. You and I…. Well, who knows what could have been?"

She swallowed hard. There was no sense in both of them being miserable. Also, if he had any reservations about returning to the seventeenth century, he might back out. And his child would never know him.

Besides, if Colin did stay in the twenty-first century, he'd surely regret leaving his wife to fend for herself and their child. That would be an even more difficult task back then than it was now.

Lying was the kindest thing she could do for him. "Nothing could have happened between us, Colin. I…have someone in my life."

Disappointment flickered over Colin's face but swiftly vanished. Straightening, he nodded. "I see."

"The guy who brought over that casserole last night, Chuck, he and I…. We're dating."

"Oh." Without another word, Colin left the room.

Her heart ached, but she had to hold her emotions in check, at least until Colin was gone.

At last, Luna coaxed Hecate into a bag-like cat carrier, and they got into the car. Colin linked his hands in his lap and stared out the window at the passing streets he'd never see again in his lifetime.

Better than looking at Luna. It pained him, more than he'd thought possible, that shortly, they'd be parted forever. She'd be no more to him than the ghost of a memory…but it was the way things had to be.

Luna parked at the waterfront. Despite the overcast sky, the area was crowded with folk enjoying the ongoing festivities. A plump, gray-haired woman waited at the bottom of the roped-off walkway that led to the museum entrance. Seeing Luna, she waved.

"You brought your cat?" Roberta asked as they approached.

"I just picked up Hecate from an appointment," Luna said. "I didn't want to leave her in the hot car." Careful not to bump the cat carrier, Luna hugged the older woman. "Roberta, this is Colin Wilshire. Colin, Roberta Millingham. She manages the archives of the Historical Society."

"A pleasure to meet you." He took Roberta's hand and kissed the backs of her age-spotted fingers.

Roberta blushed. "Goodness. A proper seventeenth-century greeting."

"Aye." Smiling, he released her hand.

"You know, you look just as I imagined the

original Colin Wilshire to look. He was, from all I've read about him, quite handsome and a bit of a rogue."

Colin's brows rose. "A rogue?"

"Oh, yes. He got caught up in a scandal and had to leave England in a hurry. Whisked his pregnant wife away in the dead of night, and off they sailed."

Good God. Her account—not entirely accurate—made him sound like an idiot. He wouldn't stand for it. "I'm a bit of an expert on Colin Wilshire, and—"

"You are? You must give a talk for our group sometime."

"I'd be happy to, but—"

"My goodness, you're even wearing historically accurate clothes. They're some of the best I've ever seen, and I've seen quite a few costumes in the twenty-two years I've volunteered for the society."

"Well, thank you—"

"Are you a historical re-enactor? Did someone in your organization make your clothes? I'd love to get the contact information from you."

He'd love to get in a word in edgewise.

"Luna, wherever did you find this charming man?"

"I found him on the beach." Luna smiled at him. "Due to unforeseen circumstances, he'd missed the reception and—"

The woman tapped her hand to her brow. "I do apologize. I get a bit carried away sometimes. I'm sorry you weren't able to join us that evening, Mr. Wilshire, because it was a splendid occasion, but I'll make sure you have plenty of time to look around the museum."

"I am most grateful," he said.

Beaming, she opened the rope barrier to let them through. "This way."

Roberta toddled ahead up the walkway while Colin followed a few paces behind, Luna in the rear. The water either side of the wooden walk grew increasingly blue-black in color. A memory scratched at the back of his mind: the vast ocean darkening to murky hues as the tempest in 1645 rolled in.

A shudder rippled through him.

Just before he boarded the ship, Luna caught his hand. Pausing, he glanced back. Her gaze solemn, she squeezed his fingers. "I know this must be difficult for you."

His throat tightened again. He nodded.

"I'm here for you. I will always...." She cleared her throat. "Well, you know."

He wasn't sure how to answer her. So, he said nothing, merely pressed her hand in return before pulling his free and stepping down onto the deck...which had been streaming with water and splitting apart the last time he'd been on it.

"I'll wait here," Roberta said, sitting on a plastic chair beside a sign that provided some information on the Guinevere. She squinted up at the sky. "The weatherman said we're in for a storm, but hopefully, it will hold off for a little while longer."

Colin walked to the opposite side of the boat, to the rail where he'd stood with the captain, and curled his fingers on the smooth section. While it had obviously been repaired, it fitted seamlessly with the rest of the rail. How glad he was that the Guinevere had been restored with care.

A raindrop landed on the back of his hand. The whisper of the breeze through the ship's new sails stirred up images of the wind ravaging the vessel long-ago; the enormous waves crashing down on the deck; the urgent shouts of the crew.

He shut his eyes, mentally wrenched back to when he'd been trying to loosen the knotted rope of the tender. He'd been terrified, but trying to act calm, because the women and children would have no chance of surviving if the men panicked—

"Colin."

He glanced over his shoulder. Luna stood near the captain's quarters. "There's a display in here. Paintings, artifacts—"

"Thanks. I'll be there in a moment."

His attention shifted to Roberta, talking in a loud voice with a man who must be down on the boardwalk. Colin's gaze slid to the doorway to the passenger cabins. A vision of Evelyn standing at the threshold, of the young girl holding her doll, flashed through his mind.

The door was closed.

He'd rather not interrupt Roberta to ask permission to go down into that part of the ship. She might say no. He couldn't be denied now.

Anticipation burning in his gut, he crossed the deck. When he tried the handle, the door opened.

Still holding the cat carrier, Luna hurried to him. "Where are you going?"

Without a word, he headed down the stairs. Once again, he heard the frightened cries and moans of the passengers. Sweat cooled on his palms, but he pressed onward, down the stuffy, shadowed hallway that smelled of beeswax polish.

A rope barred the entrance to his and Evelyn's cabin. He slipped under it and into the room that seemed smaller than he remembered. The furnishings weren't in the right places, either.

Luna stood at the rail. "Hey. Colin?"

"Let me know if Roberta comes down the stairs, will you?"

"What are you going to do?"

"If it's still here, I need to get something from this room."

"The restoration team would surely have found—"

"I still have to check."

He went to the wall and ran his fingers over the crown molding.

Luna made a sound of distress. "Colin!"

"I *have* to check," he growled.

His fingertips found the small lever, skillfully made to look like it was a natural part of the molding's design.

He pressed it.

With a muffled *click*, the molding snapped a fraction out of alignment.

He caught his breath. If his sketches weren't there….

His hand trembled. He felt a little dizzy, but he pulled the molding aside and peered into the cavity.

Inside was the wooden tube.

Chapter Seven

Luna couldn't imagine how the restoration team hadn't discovered the cylindrical container that Colin had removed from behind some molding, although this area of the ship hadn't yet been fully restored. "What is that?"

Colin held the faded wooden tube to his chest. "It was supposed to be my family's future." He carefully opened the top and pulled out a rolled-up, yellowed scroll. Meeting her gaze, he slipped it back inside.

Hecate meowed in her carrier.

Luna's heart pounded. "Do you think I should 0let her out here?"

"I don't know how this opening portals thing works."

Above their heads, the boards creaked. Then something thudded on the upper deck.

Luna could have sworn that she heard a woman's muffled shout. "What was that?" Luna tightened her grip on the cat carrier.

Colin frowned, clearly uneasy. "Roberta didn't say anything about anyone else coming on board."

Luna's witch senses ramped up. "No, she

didn't."

Thunder roared in the distance.

Luna shook her head. "I feel a weird energy now, something…." She searched for the right descriptive words. "It's anxious…and evil."

Another boom of thunder.

"Stay here," Colin ordered. "I'm going up on deck to see what's happened."

"Oh no you don't." Luna squared her shoulders. "I'm no seventeenth-century damsel in distress."

He kissed the top of her head. "I'm well aware of the formidable woman you are. And because I care deeply about you, I don't want anything to harm you."

A pleasant ache settled low in her belly. "Thank you. I feel the same way about you, so I'm coming with you."

A warm smile settled on his lips only for a moment. The worry returned to his expression just as quickly. "Stay behind me."

Luna set the carrier down, took out Hecate, and picked her up. "Just in case she has to help you get through the portal in a hurry."

Colin tucked the tube under his arm as he left the cabin. Wind howled, and the distinctive pitter-patter of rain ramped up.

Luna quickly cast a spell to protect all three of them. At the top of the narrow stairs, Luna heard a soft whimper. At the far side of the deck, she glimpsed a black shoe. Roberta's shoe.

Elbowing Colin's arm, she pointed to it.

Colin tucked Luna behind him and took a few steps toward Roberta.

Hecate vibrated with a low growl.

Suddenly, something hard and cold poked into Luna's back. Hot breath landed on her neck, making her skin crawl.

"Give me the tube," a man barked from behind her. "Unless you want me to shoot her right here."

Colin spun around, eyes blazing, rain dripping from his hair.

Hecate leaped from Luna's arms then took off across the deck and disappeared behind a display.

Hot-cold shivers racked Luna's entire body.

Goddess, protect us.

"Who are you?" Colin demanded.

"Someone with more right to that treasure than you." The man jabbed his gun against her.

One hand fisted at his side, and the other holding the tube, Colin looked at Luna before his gaze shifted beyond her. "Let her go, and we can talk about this."

The man sneered. "You're hardly in a position to negotiate, pal."

Tiny muscles around Colin's jaw ticked. "I'll give you what you want, as soon as you let her walk away."

Her legs felt weak, as if they'd buckle at any moment, but she couldn't give in to her fear. "I've already phoned the sheriff," she said. "When we were below deck. He's on his way here." Maybe the lie would give the man second thoughts about harming them.

"You're lying," he hissed. "Give me that tube." The man moved next to Luna and pointed the gun at her side.

Gulping, she looked at him. There was something familiar about him—the red hair, the mirrored sunglasses. Then it hit her—she'd seen him at her vendor booth on Founders' Day. He'd been wearing a pirate costume, with those same glasses.

The man wiped rain from his face. "Just give it to me." He cocked the trigger. "Or I give it to your girlfriend."

Colin would rather be back in the churning ocean, almost drowning, than obey the bastard threatening Luna. But, he'd never before faced a weapon like the one the man held pressed against her.

Back in England, Colin had seen flintlock pistols for sale. While the inventor in him had wanted to see how the firing mechanism worked, he hadn't bought a pistol, and not just because they were costly. He'd heard what could happen if the gunpowder and flame weren't combined properly. He wouldn't have been able to support Evelyn if he'd lost a hand, or arm, or died.

The weapon the man held somewhat resembled a pistol, but was smaller and more angular. Flintlocks only fired one shot, but weapons had changed a lot since 1645. At least, they had judging by the few programs he'd seen bits of after Luna had taught him how to use the TV remote.

To save her and poor Roberta, he must get the gun away from the man.

Not easily done.

Luna obviously understood the peril; he'd never seen her so pale.

The man snarled. "I *said*—"

"Don't hurt her. Please." Colin raised his free hand in what he hoped would be a sign of yielding.

"Hand over the tube."

"I will," Colin said. "But, if you let her go first—"

"No."

Luna visibly shivered.

"Put the tube on the deck. Roll it to me."

"All right. But, honestly, why do you care about this old container?"

The man glowered. "I could care less about the tube. I want what's inside."

How did he even know what was inside? "Is that what you believe you have a right to?" Colin asked as he slowly crouched.

"I don't just *believe* I have a right to it. I know I do."

Bastard. How dare he insist he had a claim to Colin's work?

Colin must delay passing over the tube. He had to figure out what the hell was going on. "Forgive me for not understanding." He looked up at the man. "How would you have such right? You weren't on the ship in 1645."

"My relatives were."

"Relatives?"

"Colin and Evelyn Wilshire."

Colin met Luna's shocked gaze. He barely managed to catch an oath before it could leave his lips. "You're a descendant of theirs?"

"I'm related to Colin's cousin, Matthew."

"That doesn't entitle you—"

"Yeah, it does. I have the original letters."

"Letters?"

"From Colin to Matthew. I inherited them years ago, along with some other family stuff."

Understanding bloomed in Colin's mind. The bastard had the correspondence in which Colin talked about his two-wheeled invention.

He mentally put the pieces of the puzzle together. "When you heard about the restoration of the Guinevere—"

"I knew Colin would have taken what he valued most on the ship. I tried to visit it while it was being restored. Even with credentials, I couldn't get access."

"You broke into the museum," Luna whispered.

"I didn't have a choice. I've spent *years* trying to find the sketches. I've risked my career and lost money searching for them." The man shoved the gun harder against her side, and she moaned. "Now, roll the tube—"

"Leave the slightest mark on Luna's flesh," Colin gritted, "and you will pay for it."

"You'll do what?" The man sneered. "I'm the one with the gun."

Colin tightened his grip on the container. "Tell me this. You want the sketches. Why? To sell them to a museum? To provide a better life for your family?"

"What family? I don't have kids. My wife divorced me."

Smart woman.

"My colleagues refuse to believe that my relative invented the bicycle." The man's features hardened with anger. "Once I have the sketches, I can shove the drawings in their faces. I'll show them I was right. I'll be the most sought-after historian of this century."

So he was motivated by greed.

Colin growled…and pushed the tube. Hard.

The man's foot shot out to stop the container, but it rumbled past him. He swore. As his gaze followed it, he stepped back a fraction.

Lunging to his feet, Colin shoved Luna aside then kicked the man's gun-holding hand. He yelped, but didn't lose his grip on the weapon.

Damn.

"Go!" Colin pointed to where Roberta lay. Luna would be safe there. She could also check on the woman.

Luna ran.

The man snatched up the tube and swung the gun in Luna's direction. Colin stepped between her and the gunman. The weapon pointed straight at Colin's chest.

He locked gazes with the gunman. The beat of rain on the deck, the thud of Luna's footsteps, the drumming of Colin's pulse, all faded to a poignant cognizance that here, now, he could die.

But Luna would live.

Anguish gripped Colin. One day, once the horror of this incident had faded for her, she'd find a man who deserved her. That man would marry her and provide a loving home for her and their children. She'd be cherished, treasured—and she'd be happy; happier than she'd ever been. She might even think about Colin once in a while, but her focus would be on enjoying life with her husband.

Dying was a sacrifice Colin would gladly make…because he loved her.

The truth of that realization warmed him like a

large swig of brandy.

He didn't just care about her. He loved her.

Loved the sparkle in her eyes, the way she tucked her hair back behind her ear, the expressions she made when concentrating on her baking.

If only he'd had more days with her...but maybe there'd been a reason to his being brought through time, a reason he only understood now: to save her.

The gunman's gaze sharpened. "Sorry, pal. I didn't plan for anyone to die."

He was going to fire the gun.

Colin clenched his hands. He'd die with honor, fighting—

Crash.

Across the deck, a display board had fallen over.

Hecate scrambled away from it.

Roaring, the gunman spun to face the cat.

Bang!

Wood splintered.

Luna screamed. "Colin!"

Colin lunged, locking his right arm around the gunman's neck. Spluttering, the man rammed the wooden tube into Colin's ribs. For a second, the deck became a blur, but Colin hung on.

The man made a choking sound.

"Drop the gun," Colin commanded, his mouth near the man's left ear. He increased the pressure of his arm.

The gunman flailed.

Bang!

He'd shot a hole in the railing.

With an angry hiss, Colin kicked the back of

the man's knee. As the bastard's leg gave out, Colin grabbed for the gun. The man resisted, but Colin shoved him down to the deck. Facedown, spitting with fury, the man struggled and tried to rise, but Colin knocked him back down. He wrenched the gunman's fingers open, freed the weapon, and kicked it across the deck. It disappeared under a heaped fishing net.

Colin glowered at the man, now rolling onto his back. Colin snatched the tube. "Sorry, *pal*." He kicked the gunman in the head. The man's body went limp, his eyes sliding closed.

He became aware of a woman shouting. "Colin!"

Glancing over his shoulder, he saw Luna, peering out from the safe spot. When their gazes locked, she asked, "Are you okay?"

"I'm fine."

"Hecate?"

He saw the cat huddled by the barrels. "Fine too, as far as I can tell."

Luna breathed a sob of relief.

"How is Roberta?"

"She's awake, but disoriented. I've called the police."

"Good." Colin gestured to the unconscious man. "I'll take care of him. Then I'll come help you."

Colin glanced about the deck. He saw a coil of rope on an iron hook—part of the display on rope knots that Hecate had knocked over. Colin hurried to snatch up the rope then used it to bind the man's arms behind his back and secure his ankles. The gunman wouldn't be able to stand, let alone flee.

Picking up the tube again, Colin went to where Luna crouched next to Roberta. Luna held the older woman's hand. Blood stained Roberta's neck and shoulder.

As Colin knelt next to Luna, she discreetly motioned to the back of her head. The gunman had hit Roberta there. Anger churned within Colin that the man had not only struck a woman, but one who was elderly. He truly hoped she wasn't badly hurt.

"How are you feeling?" he gently asked.

"I have a terrible headache," Roberta said with a rueful smile. "Not seeing all that well, either."

"You're being very brave," he said.

"I don't feel brave."

"Come now," Colin soothed. "Think of the tale you'll have to tell the other ladies of the Historical Society. Your grandchildren, too."

Roberta's expression brightened a fraction.

"None of them will have had such an adventure," Luna added.

"Well, that's true," Roberta said.

Thunder growled overhead, and the older woman shivered.

"Let's get you out of the rain." Colin glanced at Luna. "The captain's quarters are open, right?"

"Yes." A curious expression flickered over her features. "You really need to look at the display there."

"It's settled then." He handed Luna the tube. "Please watch over this for me. Would you mind going on ahead to hold the door?"

"Sure."

Luna took the container then Colin slid his arms under Roberta and carefully lifted her into his arms. He carried her to the captain's quarters, taking care to jostle her as little as possible.

"I can tell the others," Roberta mumbled, "that

I was in the arms of a handsome gentleman."

Colin chuckled. "That would be partly right. I do consider myself to be a gentleman."

Spying an upholstered bench that had been installed in the middle of the room so visitors could sit and leisurely study the paintings if they liked, he took Roberta over to it and laid her down. She winced as she settled on her back.

He pulled his shirt over his head. "Here."

Roberta's eyes opened. Seeing his bare chest, her eyes widened. "Oh, goodness."

Colin rolled up the garment. Leaning over her, he lifted her shoulders to tuck the makeshift pillow under her head. "I'm afraid it's damp, but hopefully you'll be more comfortable."

"That's very nice of you," Roberta said. "Won't you be cold?"

"I'll be fine."

Straightening, he glanced over at Luna. Her gaze snapped up from his naked torso.

Ha! He'd caught her ogling.

"You all right?" he asked, as her cheeks turned pink.

"Pretty much."

Water trailed from the ends of her hair, and she appeared to be soaked from head to toe. But, he'd never seen her look more beautiful. He yearned to cross to her, pull her into his arms, and kiss her until they were both breathless with desire. He longed to show her just how true and deep his feelings for her ran. But, even as he thought to go to her, he heard the distant sirens. The police were on the way.

"I should find Hecate. Can you handle things here?" Luna asked.

"Aye."

She hesitated, as though wanting to say more, but then walked outside into the rain.

Colin went to the end of the bench and sat beside Roberta. Her eyes were closed, but he sensed she wasn't unconscious, just resting.

His attention shifted to the museum display. He rose as he saw the glass case holding the tattered cloth doll—the same one the Bell daughter had been holding before the wave had crashed into him, her, and Evelyn.

Memories crowded into his mind again: the briny tang of seawater; the gut-wrenching terror; the fearful expressions of the other passengers. Many of the artifacts had been donated by relatives of those who had survived the shipwreck. The display cases featured stained leather gloves, porcelain snuff boxes, silver combs, and more. According to the placard, the water-damaged trunk in front of him, a bit larger than the one he and Evelyn had brought onto the ship, had belonged to the Harrisons.

An oil painting hung above a case of jewelry. As he focused on the woman's face, his heart froze. *Evelyn.* The painting was dated 1652, seven years after the Guinevere's sailing. That meant Evelyn had survived the storm. If she had, surely their child had as well?

He sucked in a breath, almost afraid to look at the next portrait.

His whole body tensing, Colin shifted his gaze to the painted image: A seven-year-old boy.

A lad with intelligent eyes and a mischievous smile.

A fair-haired, blue-eyed son...who was the

spitting image of Matthew.

Chapter Eight

S hock and confusion tore through Colin. The boy in the picture had to be the child Evelyn had been carrying when they were on the Guinevere.

Their son.

His son…who didn't resemble him at all.

Sickening numbness coursed through Colin as he took in the portrait to the right of the boy: a painting of Matthew. Colin could easily guess why the lad looked like Matthew.

Could what Colin suspected of his wife be true?

He started reading the card on the wall by the painting. The boy's name was Brandon Wilshire. Brandon was Colin's middle name; the name he and Evelyn had chosen for their child if he'd been a boy.

Colin's throat tightened, for after the shipwreck in which her husband had been declared missing and presumed dead, Evelyn had written to Matthew in England. She'd revealed that he, not Colin, was the father of her child. She'd always loved Matthew, but the arrangement that had bound her to Colin had forced her and Matthew to keep their affair secret. With Colin gone, they could be together for the rest of their lives. She'd begged Matthew to find her.

He'd written back expressing his true love in return and had traveled across the ocean to marry her. Evelyn had borne Matthew three more children, and they'd lived long and happy lives in Cat's Paw Cove.

Copies of their correspondence were on display in a glass case. Colin knew their handwriting. The letters were genuine.

His gaze returned to his wife's portrait. No wonder Matthew had wanted Colin to stay in England. Had Evelyn meant to tell Colin the truth about the child while they were together in their cabin, just before the tempest hit? Probably so.

Their conversation replayed in his mind.

"I was going to wait to tell you," Evelyn said.

"Tell me what?"

She drew a sharp breath. "It's…it's about—"

Evelyn had thought they'd been about to die, and she'd tried to confess to him.

She'd betrayed their marriage vows, betrayed his trust, betrayed all that they should have meant to one another…and part of him was furious that she'd treated him that way.

But, even if she'd told him the truth about their son, he'd have supported her and the boy. Colin would never have forsaken them.

Evelyn had married for love, though. She'd found happiness, and he couldn't help but be relieved and glad that all had worked out well for her.

He didn't have to go back to 1645; not if he didn't want to.

Hope bloomed within him.

Hope that for once, he had a choice in his own

CATHERINE KEAN and WYNTER DANIELS

destiny.

Did he dare to hope that his future included Luna?

Luna finished reading Evelyn and Matthew's letters in the display case. So, Colin's wife had lied to him about her pregnancy. Luna's chest constricted, knowing the betrayal he must surely feel. But would that be enough to convince him not to return to his own time?

Did she dare hope?

Tamping down a flicker of optimism, she glanced up at him.

Colin leaned against a post, his face an unreadable mask of warring emotions.

Hecate bumped against Colin's shin and yowled over and over.

He stared at Luna. "What do you think she wants?"

Picking up the cat, Luna held her to her chest. "What is it, little one?"

Hecate wriggled out of Luna's arms and ran to a closed door near the displays. She pawed the wall then sat down there.

Luna and Colin closed the distance to the spot. Colin tried the handle, but it was locked.

Hecate bumped her nose to the wood. The door shimmered and morphed into what looked like a high definition television screen. Through the opening, they could see a stormy sea, hear the howling wind, and even feel the sea spray.

The portal!

Colin gasped.

Luna's chest ached. But she couldn't stop him from returning to his time if that was what he wanted. If he did go back, she'd mourn him for the rest of her life, for what could have been. Yet she couldn't bring herself to voice her opposition. Colin had to do whatever he thought he should.

Tears stung her eyes. She took his hand. "How do you know you'll survive the storm?"

He faced her. "I don't."

The sirens grew louder. "Help is here," Luna said. Her pulse pounding, she glanced through a small window to see several uniformed paramedics and deputies heading toward the ship.

Luna started to touch Colin's cheek, but at the last moment, withdrew her hand. "If you're going to leave—"

"I'm not.… Unless, of course, you'd prefer to be with someone else?"

Although Chuck was a nice man, she knew she'd have never grown her feelings for him, even if she hadn't met Colin. "Never," Luna whispered.

Colin drew her into his arms and kissed her. "Then my life…my new life…is here. With you."

Hecate meowed and rubbed against Luna's leg, purring loudly.

The portal shrank then closed up and became a plain old door again.

Colin held Luna's face in his hands. "This is where I belong, Luna, with you."

He was staying. She could hardly breathe. Her heart fluttered, and she felt as if she'd just drunk several glasses of champagne.

"Is everyone okay down there?" a deputy called from the upper deck.

Colin tipped his chin toward the entrance. "We should—"

"Yup." Drawing a deep breath, she picked up Hecate and she and Colin headed out of the cabin to join the officers and paramedics. "There's an injured lady in the captain's quarters."

"The scoundrel responsible is out cold," Colin added.

Minutes later, they told Sheriff Higgins what had transpired—leaving out the part about a portal opening to the past.

"I'll need that tube." Sheriff Higgins tipped his chin toward the cylinder under Colin's arm.

"That belongs to me," the thug muttered as two paramedics lifted him onto a stretcher.

"Actually, I believe it's the property of the Historical Society." RJ held out his hand. "May I?"

Colin's jaw ticked, but after a few seconds, he gave it to Sheriff Higgins.

When Luna thought to protest, Colin squeezed her hand. "It's all right. I have more important things to think about right now."

Like her? She could hardly hold back a smile.

What choice had Colin had, though? He hardly could have explained to the sheriff that the tube belonged to Colin because he was a time traveler.

"What's the attacker's name?" Luna asked RJ.

The sheriff glanced down at the small tablet in his right hand. "He says it's Otis Wilshire, but who knows? I'd like the two of you to come to my office and give a statement. It can wait until morning, though. Sounds like you two have been through it today."

Luna nodded. "Of course. How's Roberta doing?"

The sheriff's lips flattened. "She agreed to go to the hospital to be checked out. How anyone could attack a sweet old lady like her is beyond me."

"Only a scoundrel would do such a thing." Colin dried off with the towel a paramedic had given him.

"I couldn't agree more," RJ said. "Rest assured, Otis—or whoever he is—will get what's coming to him."

"Thank you, Sheriff." Colin shook hands with RJ.

"You're new in town, aren't you?" Sheriff Higgins asked Colin.

Luna slipped her arm around Colin's waist. "He's from England."

Colin drew her closer. "I'll be staying, though."

Luna's heart felt so full. She couldn't remember ever being this happy before.

Luna parked the car at her cottage and switched off the engine. She studied Colin, her expression thoughtful. "What was in the tube, if you don't mind my asking?"

He hesitated, but after what she'd endured today, Luna deserved to know. "The sketches of my two-wheeled invention."

"The bicycle," she said.

"Aye."

"I see." After a silence, she asked, "Are you

upset the sheriff took the tube? Is that why you hardly said a word on the drive here?"

"I've been thinking." Truth be told, from the second Colin had handed over his drawings, he'd been mulling what that meant for his future with Luna. She deserved happiness, love, and the security of knowing he'd never knowingly disappoint or hurt her in any way. Yet, within five minutes of him retrieving the tube, her life had been in danger.

If the incident on the Guinevere had turned out differently, she could have been shot and killed. He'd have never forgiven himself if she'd died because of his sketches—and he'd not allow her life to be endangered because of them ever again.

Uncertainty touched her gaze. "Have you changed your mind about going through the portal?"

"Not at all." He caught her hand and brushed his thumb over her fingers.

"What is it, then?"

He glanced out the car's front window, at the rain still falling but not as intensely now. "I can't help wondering how many other people, besides Otis, know about my drawings."

"There's no way of finding out," she said.

"That's what worries me. All has ended well for now, but—"

"Colin, you can't torment yourself with what-ifs."

"I can." He couldn't keep his tone from roughening. "I have to. You are everything to me, and I…."

Her eyes glistening, she leaned over and kissed him. "You are everything to me, too."

"If you are all right with it, I'd like to join the

Historical Society."

"Of course I'm all right with it." Luna smiled. "Roberta will be thrilled."

A wry smile tugged at his lips. "I assure you, I'm not joining to delight Roberta. If I become an integral part of the organization, I'll be able to keep track of my drawings. With luck, I'll help determine what happens to them once they've been authenticated. I expect in this century, there's tecknolagee that can confirm my sketches are several hundred years old."

Luna nodded.

"If my drawings become part of the exhibition on the Guinevere," he continued, "I can watch over them and all of the other items on display. I'll monitor the portal, too."

"Yes. That would be a good idea." She frowned. "Do you think someone—or something—might come through that portal to Cat's Paw Cove?"

"As you said, in this town, anything is possible."

"It sure is." She winked. "I still don't understand how you got here, but I'm very glad you did."

"I am too," he murmured. Desire stirred. He'd love to show her just how glad he was.

Her gaze narrowed, not with wariness, but coyness. "That's quite a look, Mr. Wilshire."

He must replicate his 'look' in front of the bathroom mirror, so he'd understand what she was seeing now. "What do you mean?" he drawled.

A lovely flush spread over her face. "You're staring at me as though you're starving, and I'm a giant plate of lemon bars."

He fought not to chuckle. "Is that so terrible?"

"No." She sucked in a quick breath. "I think it's perfect."

He slowly grinned. Perhaps he should go change into the jeans he'd worn before. She might help him with the zipper again. For starters.

She tsked. "Colin Wilshire."

"Colin *Brandon* Wilshire," he corrected. His wicked mind teased him with the idea of licking powdered sugar off her bare skin. *Aye.* He reached for the door handle.

Luna got out of the car and opened the rear door to get out Hecate's carrier.

"I'll meet you inside," Colin said.

"I'll be waiting." With a saucy sway of her hips, Luna went into the house.

Colin smiled and, as light rain landed on his hair and clothes, he looked toward the ocean, happiness soaring within him.

He'd traveled through time and found Luna, his adorable little witch.

At last, he was home.

Three weeks later….

Luna pulled a pan of cinnamon buns out of the oven and put it on a cooling rack. Before she'd removed her oven mitt, Colin came in the back door of the café carrying a metal contraption that resembled a doll-size Ferris wheel.

"Morning, beautiful. Already hard at work,

hmm?" He set his burden in the corner then came over and swept Luna off her feet for a toe-curling kiss.

With her hair pulled up in a hairnet, and wearing her favorite old apron, Luna was sweaty and dusted in flour and powdered sugar, but she'd never felt more attractive. Because Colin always treated her like the most desirable woman in the world.

When he finally released her, she was breathless from the kiss, but tingling with happiness from head to toe. She pulled off her oven mitt and tipped her chin toward the metal wheel. "Another invention?"

Colin nodded excitedly. "This one is for the cats."

"Oh?" She couldn't wait to see what it did. Colin had already made her life easier with his automated icing machine that allowed Luna to frost two dozen cinnamon buns or cupcakes with the press of a button. He'd also built her friend Fiona a rotating display rack for the crystals at the Cheshire Apothecary. And thanks to the news story on CPC-TV and in the *Cat's Paw Cove Courier* about how Colin had rescued poor Roberta Millingham, and discovered the now-famous sketches of an early bicycle prototype, Colin had become a bit of a local hero. Someone from the Chamber of Commerce had contacted him about fixing some of the antique pulleys that worked the stone monoliths at Coquina Castle. He now had a waiting list of people who wanted to hire him to fix items no one else could.

"Jordan told me that cats rarely drink enough water," Colin said. "And that can cause health problems for them."

"Is it a water wheel?" she asked.

Colin grinned. "It is. I read on the computer that cats enjoy drinking from faucets and other sources of running water. The wheel will circulate water in two fountains. Maybe the cats will drink more."

"Ingenious!"

She gave him a quick kiss before returning to her baking.

A while later, Colin returned to the kitchen. "It's all set up. Do you have time to check it out?"

Luna glanced into the café. Leo had the front under control. "Sure."

Colin led her into the cat room.

Jordan was sitting on a beanbag chair, holding one of the older cats, a striped tabby. "Hey, Luna." She giggled like a little girl.

Why did Jordan seem so giddy? "Excited about Colin's new invention?" Luna asked her friend.

Jordan laughed. "Yeah, that's it."

"Okay."

"Over here," Colin said. Draping his arm around Luna's shoulders, he gestured at two identical cat fountains separated by the slow-moving wheel. He clicked a toggle switch and the fountains turned on.

"Cool!" she said.

Suddenly, she heard a clink. Had a screw or a nut come loose? Leaning closer to see into the fountain on the right, she noticed something sparkling inside. "What is that?"

"See if you can reach it," Colin said.

Jordan came over wearing a huge smile. "What is it, Luna?"

On the side of the fountain, she found a glittering ring. She gasped and looked at Colin.

"The stone is sea glass." He reached into the

well for the ring then kneeled before her and took her left hand. "Luna Halpern, I realize that by today's standards, this is awfully quick. But I know what I know. I love you, and I want to spend the rest of my life making you happy."

Her entire body hummed with surprise and excitement and delight. Her lips moved, but she couldn't manage a single word.

Hopping up and down, Jordan hugged her from behind. "Yes, she says yes!"

All Luna could do was nod.

"You have to say it for yourself, Luna." Colin chuckled. "Although I appreciate your help, Jordan."

Sucking in a shaky breath, she nodded again. "Yes, yes, yes."

He scooped her into his arms, lifted her off the ground, and kissed her.

Colin was right. When you know, you know.

Want more Cat's Paw Cove?
Turn the page to read an excerpt from Wynter
Daniels' book *Her Homerun Hottie*.
Available now!

Event Planner and earthly Cupid Tori Sutherland enjoys nothing more than playing matchmaker for lonely hearts. Too bad Tori will never find her own happy-ever-after because the only guy she ever loved moved on years ago.

Heath Castillo managed to escape his dysfunctional family for a career in major-league baseball. His only regret was not acting upon his desire for his best friend. When an injury threatens his livelihood, Heath has no choice but to face the ghosts of his past.

When long-buried passions ignite, Heath and Tori consider taking a chance on love. But will the forces that kept them apart in high school destroy their budding romance before it even begins?

Available in eBook and print.

Chapter One

"How bad was the damage?" Tori Sutherland cradled the phone between her shoulder and ear as she stared into her rearview mirror and smoothed on pink lipstick. She checked that her hair looked presentable but her curls, as usual, weren't behaving. It wasn't every day she was summoned to appear before the town council. Heaven help her.

"I don't even know where to begin," Alexa said. "Apparently the bride's relatives are no strangers to the penal system. One of the gazillion uncles was yelling, 'I ain't afraid to go back to prison,' as the cops hauled him out of the banquet room. And his wife was cursing a blue streak, telling him she was going to kick his ass for ruining the wedding. Soon as she bailed him out. Then the groomsman who cut his arm on the glass from the window tells me it won't stop bleeding. I promise I'll clean up the blood from the seat in the van. Couldn't be helped."

Tori prayed the fiasco wouldn't be the downfall of her party planning business. Bad enough she still owed her mother more than half the startup capital she'd borrowed from her. If Cat Town Events went under, she'd be indebted to her mom forever. She shuddered as she put on her earrings just as the stoplight turned green. "Is the groomsman okay? How'd the window get broken?"

"He's fine. No worries. Only took five stitches." Alexa drew an audible breath. "They broke the window during the melee. Two guys got into it over a girl they'd both dated. Or were still dating. Anyway, one punch led to another. It was the man who tried to break up the fight that got cut. Glass went everywhere from the chair someone threw."

Tori shut her eyes a moment and wished this was all a dream. Who were these people, the Hatfields and McCoys? "The chair?" Although she really didn't want to know.

"The one that went through the window" Alexa clarified. "Are you paying attention, boss?"

"I am. I'm just hoping that the newlyweds can survive the turmoil of future family gatherings. It sounds as if they both have lots of nuts on their respective family trees." As an earthly Cupid, Tori took her gift of matchmaking very seriously. So far, all the couples she'd brought together were still happily coupled, but this latest pair might just put Tori's supernatural power to the test. She turned her van onto Tabby Road and brushed white cat hair from her lapels. Which really showed against her red blazer. Time to step up her search for a permanent home for all the cats she'd been fostering. "Promise me something, Alexa."

"Anything."

"Next time a client wants to use a city property for their wedding, sweet sixteen, bar mitzvah, or whatever, we say no." Too bad that it cost so much less for the use of the community room at city hall than any of the private venues in Cat's Paw Cove.

"Maybe that's why the council wants to see you. To ask you not to use their place anymore."

"I wish." If that were why she'd been summoned to the meeting this morning, she'd get on her knees after and kiss the sidewalk in front of the town hall. But she suspected the reason was way more serious, something that had the potential to ruin her. What if they forced her to surrender her occupational license or told her she could no longer plan events in the town limits? Her name was on the rental agreement, and she was the responsible party. Good grief. She never took a dime for her matchmaking services. The event planning business was her only source of income. She stared at her reflection and tried to rub away the lines creasing her forehead. "I'd better go. Can't be late for my execution."

"I'm so sorry I can't be there with you. It took me three weeks to get this dental appointment and—"

"Alexa, it's okay. I'll call you after the meeting." What if the council really did plan to put her out of business? What would she do? The company was just squeaking by, but if they managed to fulfill all their contracts, they'd be flush by the end of next year. Maybe even turn a profit for the first time. She couldn't imagine what it would be like to not have to worry about money.

She'd spent the last four years building her business into the premiere event planning service in the area. The only one, actually. Hopefully, the town council would take that into account. Cat Town Events filled an important role in the community. And provided gainful employment for Tori and her three assistants.

So many things had gone wrong lately, though, from a mix-up with a caterer that mistakenly served pork spare ribs at Joshua Gold's bar mitzvah, to a miscommunication with a chair rental company that left the seventy guests attending the mayor's baby shower standing for the entire party, to this latest fiasco with yesterday's wedding.

Tori's stomach roiled. She tried to scare up a positive attitude as she drove toward the Cat's Paw Cove town hall.

"I am a professional. I am intelligent and capable." But the affirmations she'd been practicing for weeks—ever since she read Empower Me, the latest self-help book—did nothing to lessen the dread churning in her stomach.

Not only had yesterday's wedding guests damaged public property, but they'd cost the taxpayers money in the form of manpower and even jail space. Maybe the council was going to demand a hefty fine from her. Which she'd likely never collect from the guilty parties. Perhaps the council would withhold all her pending party permits. No sense torturing herself with all the awful possibilities. Soon enough she'd learn what god-awful punishment they planned to mete out.

Her business was all she had. Despite the fact that she had an otherworldly gift to help others find romance, her own love life was a disaster. So she'd thrown herself into her career, and it had been going really well. Until a couple of months ago.

"I am intelligent and capable." Bolstering her courage, she pushed through the double doors to the assembly room. The seating area, which could accommodate a crowd of about a hundred, was nearly empty except for a short man in a black suit and two women.

Tori's temples started aching when she recognized one of the women as Vivi Craig, still as tall, thin and blonde as she'd been in high school. Was she still as mean as she'd been back then? Vivi and her friends had made Tori's middle and high school experience hell. Not a day had passed without one of them poking fun at or otherwise torturing the brainiac as they'd called her.

Last Tori had heard, the beautiful bully was happily divorced from a wealthy, older man. And living in Miami. So why was she here, hundreds of miles away?

Could Vivi have something to do with why the council had summoned Tori? If so, Tori was a goner for sure.

One of the council members was saying something about raising parking violation fees when Tori took a seat on the opposite side of the room from Vivi, a few seats down from the guy in the suit, who looked familiar, although she couldn't place how she knew him.

"Ah, Miss Sutherland," Deputy Mayor Quincy said. He was a sweet man in a grandfatherly way with thick gray hair, which contrasted with his deeply tanned skin. With him sitting down, no one would ever guess he stood about six feet tall. She'd run into him several times at her mom's church functions, where he'd flirted with her completely-oblivious mother. Maybe Tori would have to work some of her magic on her mom. The last time Tori had offered, her mother had insisted that she was still in mourning for Tori's dad.

"Thanks for coming on such short notice," Mr. Quincy said.

Tori tried for a smile, which didn't come easy considering she was about as thrilled to be there as she would a pap smear appointment.

The group finished their parking meter discussion then the deputy mayor opened a manila folder and shuffled a few papers around. He furrowed his brow and pinned her with a slightly frightening scowl. "Miss Sutherland, it's come to our attention that we have a big problem on our hands."

Oh crap, here it comes.

She swallowed hard, mentally rehearsing the rebuttal she'd been kicking around on the way over. Councilman Reynolds's seeing-eye dog—a golden retriever, named Icarus—panted. Was the animal was as uncomfortably warm as Tori suddenly was?

"I'm sure you've heard about the Cat's Paw Cove Tricentennial celebration, which is coming in about two weeks," Quincy said.

What did that have to do with the Palmer-Fox wedding? "Yes, Mr. Quincy."

He took a white handkerchief from his pocket and wiped beads of sweat from his forehead. "Yes, well, we had a committee working on putting together all the events. The members of which were all recommended by Councilwoman Barclay." He frowned at Rita Barclay who was seated on the far right and appeared to be engrossed in a spot on the desk that she scratched with a hot pink fingernail.

"But that's neither here nor there," Quincy said. "Point is the committee had a falling out."

Someone's phone buzzed. One of the other council members let out a nervous cough as he hit a few buttons on his cell then shoved it into his jacket pocket. "Sorry."

The deputy mayor continued. "Actually it was more than a falling out. More like World War III. Unfortunately, they hadn't finalized a single detail about the events. And now we've got no opening ceremony, gala or picnic. None of those things are going to happen unless someone who knows what the heck they're doing takes over."

Tori let out the breath she'd been holding and with it, all the tension she'd been schlepping around all morning. Thank goodness they weren't pulling the plug on her business. Quite the contrary. If they gave her the task, she could show the locals firsthand what a killer party she threw. She couldn't buy that kind of advertising. This event was way bigger than anything she'd ever handled before.

Her pulse kicked up a few notches. If the council gave her the job it could make her year—hell, it could be the difference between Cat Town Events' success or failure.

Before she could tell the mayor she'd love to take over such a huge project, Vivi jumped to her feet. "Excuse me, Mayor Quincy, but shouldn't the city take bids on this job?"

Mr. Quincy cleared his throat. "It's Deputy Mayor," he told Vivi. "I'm filling in for Mayor Lancaster while she's on maternity leave."

Vivi gave him a half nod. "Yes, well, my fiancé is now in the event planning business, just like Miss Sutherland." She tipped her perfect chin in Tori's direction, both acknowledging and dismissing her in one fell swoop.

So that was why Vivi had come. Tori resisted

the urge to run from the room. Hell no. She wasn't the geeky overweight kid she'd been in school, and she refused to let the likes of Vivi Craig kick her around ever again. For once in her life, she had an opportunity to get the better of Vivi. And more importantly, she needed this job. She knew darn well that she had the only established event planning business within thirty miles. Rather than play that card for the moment, she stood, determined to appear more professional than Vivi.

I am confident and capable.

Tori sat up taller. "Mr. Deputy Mayor, would you elaborate on what you have in mind for the town's Tricentennial?"

"Certainly." He fumbled through his file folder. "The opening ceremony will be held in the gardens at the Sherwood House on the twenty-third. We want lots of balloons and a large tent in case the weather doesn't hold. And fireworks. We'll use the community center for the gala the next night, which will be catered and have a cash bar. Then we'll put on a big picnic at Boardwalk Park on the twenty-fifth. Hot dogs, cotton candy, that sort of thing."

Vivi stepped into the aisle, all long legs, designer suit, and sleek blonde tresses. "I'd love to have an opportunity to bid on the job. Er, I mean my fiancé would."

Quincy narrowed his eyes at Vivi. "Who's your fiancé?"

Vivi served up her perfect smile as she swept her gaze over every member of the council. "Buzz Chandler." She pushed through the low swinging gate and proceeded to set a business card on the desk in front of each councilperson. "We met through my sister, who owns the most successful florist in Miami. Buzz was her supplier." She sighed. "And the rest is history."

Did she have to be as freaking perky and perfect from behind as she was from the front? Tori folded her arms over her chest, suddenly just as self-conscious about her D-cup breasts and her wide hips as she'd been in high school.

Buzz Chandler, huh? Why hadn't she ever heard of him? Wasn't as if Cat's Paw Cove was some giant metropolis. If there were another event planner in town, she'd have known about him. Last thing she needed was competition. "Buzz isn't local, Vivi, is he?"

Vivi spun around and narrowed her cat-shaped eyes on Tori, but she didn't say a word.

"Yes, Ms. Craig. I'd like to know that, too," Quincy said.

Vivi fisted her delicate hands at her sides. "He's currently living and working in West Palm Beach, but he plans to move here after we get married in the fall. So he will be local, then. Besides, isn't it protocol to have a bidding procedure rather than just hand out contracts to…" She glanced over her shoulder at Tori and flared her nostrils. "Well, to whatever ragtag company happens to ask first?"

Ragtag company? Tori bit at a hangnail, hating that she still let Vivi get to her after all these years.

She had to get the job. Despite the fact that it was way more than she'd ever done before, a much bigger job than she was used to. But how much harder could it be to plan something for a few thousand as opposed to a few hundred?

Standing taller, she smoothed down her frizzy hair. Her mother's voice played in her head.

You need to keep that mop of yours flat-ironed. And stand up straight. You only make your tummy stick out more when you slouch.

Tori squared her shoulders and sucked in her gut. Why hadn't she taken the time to straighten her hair? "My company is currently Cat's Paw Cove's only event planning service, Mr. Quincy."

"Hmm." Quincy pursed his lips. "I think we need to suspend the whole bids process just this once since we're in a pickle and that will only take more time." He glanced left then right at the council members. "Would someone make a motion?"

The council voted unanimously to award the job to Cat Town Events.

"Sorry, Ms. Craig," he said to Vivi.

Tori schooled a victorious grin from her face.

Vivi threw her a death stare then turned on her heel and marched out of the room. Tori resisted the urge to applaud.

The man in the suit seated near her mumbled something under his breath before getting up and leaving. Strange.

An elderly female clerk approached the desk and handed the deputy mayor a pink message slip. He stared at it a moment then grinned. "We just got word that our first choice for the guest of honor has accepted our invitation. Our very own native son, baseball legend Heath Castillo."

Tori nearly gasped aloud. Heath Castillo. He'd been one of her dearest childhood friends. And the only reason she watched every Angels game she could. The guy who'd taken one of his final exams early in college so he could attend her high school graduation.

The first man who broke my heart.

Oh God, could she handle being with him for three days? They'd exchanged a few emails, sent annual holiday cards, but she hadn't seen him in nearly a decade. With good reason. All these years later, she was still embarrassed about how she'd come on to him. Or more specifically, how he'd rejected her.

Was it too late to refuse the job? This was her opportunity to admit that the Tricentennial was more than she could handle. Her temples started throbbing. Giving up the job would mean it would go to Vivi's man by default. Vivi would love that. She'd rub Tori's nose in it, and worse, Vivi's fiancé's event planning service would snag tons of potential clients from the experience. Hadn't Vivi and her cohorts inflicted enough damage in Tori's life back in high school? No, she couldn't refuse the contract. Somehow she'd pull it together.

She collected the folder with the rest of the details before leaving city hall. All the way to her office, all she could think about was Heath. His all-encompassing hugs that lifted her off the ground, his deep, gravelly voice and good-natured sense of humor. Not to mention his eye candy status. With those broad shoulders and the most piercing amber eyes she'd ever seen, it was no wonder he dated the hottest models and actresses in the country.

Ten years ago she'd somehow convinced herself that her crush on him was mutual. They'd gone out after her graduation, and she'd thrown herself at him only to have him turn her down—the single most humiliating experience of her life. Not that she blamed Heath for rejecting her. She'd been a chubby, frizzy-haired klutz with a crazy fantasy that the hot star of his college baseball team would want to kiss her. She shuddered at the memory as she drove along Bent Tail Boulevard.

Four years ago, he'd sent the most beautiful flower arrangement for her dad's funeral. But how could she face him after she'd come onto him?

Every time she watched Heath play ball on TV or saw his picture in some celebrity magazine, he seemed to get better looking. He was such a big star now, he'd probably forgotten what a fool she'd made of herself. Women must throw themselves at him all the time now. Who wouldn't have a crush on the guy?

Not that she did, not anymore. Hell no. She'd been cured. After William had dumped her last year—and moved on to blonder pastures—she was through with men, at least for the time being. No way would she offer up her heart again, not after having it smashed to bits. If only her supernatural matchmaking powers worked on her, but they didn't. In fact, she was so bad at the whole dating thing, she was sure that she'd never find her own slice of happiness.

She parked behind her office and ticked off all the parties she had to cover in the next few weeks. Even with Alexa's help, this was going to be quite a challenge to pull off. Maybe she could have her deal with Heath. But they had Alexa's cousin's wedding the same weekend, and Alexa had handled it from the beginning.

There was no avoiding Heath. A shiver raced up her spine. Just nervous energy.

She hadn't seen him in person since his celebrity had skyrocketed. The idea of hosting a baseball superstar must be what had her in a dither. Nothing more. People were counting on her. She couldn't back out, not after she'd stood up to Vivi to get the job.

Despite her personal terror both at seeing Heath again and handling the biggest event she'd ever taken on, she was going to get through this. She had to. Hopefully, the ordeal wouldn't kill her!

Read the rest of Tori and Heath's story in Wynter Daniels' book *Her Homerun Hottie*, available now in eBook and print.

Turn the page to read an excerpt from Catherine Kean's next book *Hot Magic*. Pre-order now. Releases December 10

While clearing out her late mother's home in Cat's Paw Cove, Florida, Molly Hendrickson finds an unusual antique necklace. Wearing it makes her feel confident and sexy—things she hasn't felt since her ex broke off their engagement or, really, ever. She decides to keep the jewel but takes other items to Black Cat Antiquities, the local antique store, to have them appraised.

Lucian Lord, a reincarnated 12th century knight, moved to Cat's Paw Cove after a scandal in which he revealed his magical abilities to his former girlfriend. Demoted by his superiors, he's running the antiques shop while his grandfather is on vacation. But, when Molly brings in artifacts tainted by dark magic, Lucian is duty-bound to find and contain the dangerous energy before it wreaks havoc not only on the town, but the world.

Living by the knightly code of honor, Lucian vows to help Molly, especially when he realizes the necklace is the source of the ancient magic he's hunting. He's determined to save his headstrong damsel and redeem his tarnished reputation—but first, things will get very, very hot.

Available in eBook and print.

Chapter One

Cat's Paw Cove, Florida
July, Present Day

"I *wish* that woman would stop moaning."

In the midst of hanging a gilt-framed watercolor on the wall of Black Cat Antiquities, Lucian Lord glanced at the long-haired, orange and white cat sitting nearby—the feline who'd just spoken in a refined British accent.

"The Lady of the Plate can't help it, Galahad," Lucian said, as the feline jumped up onto the upholstered seat of a Victorian chair. The plaintive moan, coming from the shelf of porcelain plates at the back of the store, started up again. "Remember what my grandfather told us?"

Galahad huffed. "Yeah, yeah, she cries when there's a change in barometric pressure."

"Yes, and—"

"Since it's summer in Florida and the rainy season, she'll likely be wailing a lot. Lucky us."

Lucian fought not to smile. So, Galahad *had*

been listening to the conversation, even though at the time he'd been wild-eyed and attacking a pink toy mouse filled with catnip.

"We should have been smart and gone on that cruise with your grandfather and his lady friend. But, no. You agreed to mind the shop. How bloody chivalrous of you."

Lucian returned his attention to the painting. As Galahad well knew, Lucian had agreed to look after the store because he owed his grandfather, and not just for his help with Lucian's recent work crisis. The man had taken twelve-year-old Lucian in and raised him after the horrific car accident in which his parents had died.

Galahad excelled at complaining, but to be fair, he hadn't always been a cat. In truth, he was a reincarnated thirteenth-century squire, a lord's heir, whose ancestors had hailed from Nottinghamshire, England.

Hard to believe some days—not just the reincarnation part, but that Galahad was in fact fifteen years old and not four.

"If I had known about the Lady of the Plate, I might have stayed in Boston," Galahad groused. "I would never have moved with you to this humid, alligator-infested, mosquito-breeding swampland."

"That's not a fair description of Cat's Paw Cove."

"Alligators do live in the lake down the road. Your grandfather said so."

"He did." Lucian straightened the painting.

"And the mosquitoes—"

"And the Sherwood cats." Lucian stole a glance at Galahad. "You got quite excited about meeting female kitties who have ancestral ties to Nottinghamshire, as you do."

Galahad growled.

Lucian grinned. "Admit it, you were as intrigued to start afresh here as I was."

Indeed, moving to the seaside tourist town, with a long-term goal of taking ownership of the antique shop once his grandfather had retired, had sounded ideal weeks ago, when Lucian's life had gone to hell from one day to the next.

The moan came again from the rear of the store. The sound of a soul in torment, the wail started softly and then rose in volume. "Ooooooooooo...."

"That cry gives me the creeps." Galahad's puffed-up tail, swishing to and fro, resembled the fluffy duster stowed under the store counter.

Shaking his head, Lucian took a few backward steps and studied the watercolor in relation to the other artifacts around it. Light streaming in through the shop's long front windows shifted as people outside walked past. Thankfully, the passersby wouldn't be able to hear the Lady of the Plate's cries. Even if they caught some of Lucian and Galahad's conversation, they'd just hear a man talking to his cat, who had responded with meowing. Only the rare few gifted— or in Lucian and Galahad's case, cursed—with ancient magic could hear sounds made by magical items or understand what the feline was really saying.

"Ooooooooooo...."

Galahad's ears flattened. "Can't you shut her up? Cats *do* have a far superior sense of hearing to humans."

That could well be true. However, Galahad was always claiming ways in which felines were far superior to their human masters.

"Grandfather said she doesn't cry for long." Moving forward, Lucian nudged the painting's right edge a little higher.

Galahad growled again. "Make her stop, or I might report you for torture of a Familiar."

What? Lucian frowned at the cat. "Don't be ridiculous."

The feline's eyes gleamed. "I am quite serious."

"I spoil you rotten. I feed you that expensive, organic cat food you like twice a day. You can eat dry kibble—"

"That looks like rabbit poop—"

"—whenever you like." Lucian scowled. "And I clean your litter box several times a day and brush you every morning."

Galahad started washing a front paw.

"You haven't puked up a single hairball since I started the brushing. And, as far as I know, you haven't had any more diarrhea or digestive issues—"

"God, Lucian!"

"—since you ate the ribbon around that stack of old postcards and I had to take you to the vet."

The cat averted his gaze. "You know I couldn't help what happened with the ribbon."

"You just *had* to gobble it down."

"Yes! It looked *so* enticing." Galahad sighed. "I wish I could explain how it called to me like a siren, seducing my willpower and—"

"Yeah, well, surely my rushing you to Dr. Anderson's clinic and paying the four-hundred-and-fifty dollar vet bill showed I care about your wellbeing?"

Galahad grumbled. "You are never going to let

me forget that incident, are you?"

"Nope. And, you are never getting the chance to eat ribbon again."

"Sometimes, I can't stand to think that you and I are cursed to be together *forever*."

"Oooooooooo…."

"That's it!" The cat leapt down from the chair. "I'm going to break that damned plate. Then, she will be quiet."

"All right." The soles of Lucian's brogues squeaked on the hardwood floor as he swiveled to face the shelf and lifted his right hand, palm up. He focused his thoughts upon the exquisitely hand-painted Wagner plate portraying a beautiful, young woman with flowing brown hair and wide blue eyes.

"Shh," he silently commanded and curled his fingers inward, as though to catch and contain the sound.

The lady's mouth closed. Caught in Lucian's spell, her gaze became lifeless, as though there was no more to her than layers of paint on porcelain.

"Ahh," Galahad said. "Finally."

Lucian retrieved the etched stemware and figurines he'd moved from the shelf near the watercolor and set them back in their places. To be honest, the Lady of the Plate *had* gotten on his nerves, but because he pitied her. Like the gallant knight he'd once been centuries ago, before he'd been cursed, he hated to hear a woman in distress. The antique, like many others in the shop, bore the ghostly fragment of what had once been a flesh-and-blood person who'd died under tragic circumstances.

The first time he'd touched the plate, its provenance had flashed like snippets of film in his mind: the shrieking winds of a hurricane; an oak tree crashing through the roof of an upscale Florida home and crushing the screaming woman inside; and the plate, knocked by a branch onto a rug on the floor, intact but a silent witness to the tragedy.

When the woman had died, a piece of her soul had become connected to the antique. Most likely, she'd had a strong sentimental attachment to it.

"Would it be possible to wrap up the plate and ship it off to your brother's antiques store in London?" Galahad asked.

"You know we can't do that." Lucian picked up the hammer he'd used earlier. "Rules, remember? The curse became attached to the item here in Florida. So it belongs here in this store, with us."

Galahad stomped across the Persian carpet. "Well, thanks to Little Miss Moaning, my hopes of a much-needed afternoon nap have been destroyed. I'll be cranky for the rest of the day. *Not* my fault."

Lucian brushed cat hair off the Victorian chair. "Even if I could send the plate away, I wouldn't. Grandfather has quite a fondness for the young lady."

"Unfortunately," Galahad muttered.

"She's one of my favorites among those I call our long-term guests." Lucian's grandfather had encouraged him to take the plate from its lacquered display stand. "I got her from a guy who'd bought her shortly after Hurricane Andrew. Remember that storm back in 1992? It caused lots of damage in South Florida. Killed quite a few people, too."

The older man had taken the antique from Lucian. Gently, he'd set it back on its stand, in its assigned place on the shelf next to the Steiff teddy bear that had belonged to a mass murderer from Orlando;

the music box that had concealed the chopped off pinkie of a former trapeze artist for the Ringling Brothers Circus; and other items tainted by magic. So many tagged and catalogued items of dark magic lined the back shelves, his grandfather could claim to have a small museum.

Carrying out a specific pattern of movements with his fingers, Lucian's grandfather had reinstalled the magical field around the plate. The field not only made the antique invisible to visitors to the store, but prevented the dark energy from influencing anything—or any*one*—in the normal world. It was among the safeguards required by The Experts, that all antiques brought into the store that possessed by evil magic had to be contained in that manner.

Lucian's gaze shifted to Galahad, now sitting in one of the front windows. "Next time, try to be patient with the Lady of the Plate, okay? She isn't to blame for her curse."

"Like you and I, my lord."

Galahad rarely bothered to address Lucian that way anymore. The formality between them had become irrelevant long ago.

Centuries ago.

How Lucian wished he could recall the battle with the sorceress that had made him and Galahad into who they were today. But, he had no memories beyond his lifetime as Lucian Lord.

Galahad, though, remembered everything. He'd said the fight had taken place when Lucian was a medieval lord and Galahad his squire. Lucian had rescued his betrothed from being burned alive by the sorceress trying to attain eternal life, but before the evil bitch had died, she'd placed a curse upon Lucian's bloodline.

Immediately after she'd perished, he'd been confronted by The Experts—a secret society of sorcerers of good magic—who had given him one choice: swear allegiance to them, or be destroyed. They wouldn't allow him to fall under the influence of the ambitious, evil Dealers of Darkness. Fearing he'd never see his lady love again, Lucian had taken the oath.

For centuries, Lucian had lived, died, and been reincarnated. Each lifetime had been spent as an antiques specialist with an interest in the Middle Ages who reported to The Experts. Galahad, who'd somehow been transformed into a cat when the sorceress tried to kill him, had also lived numerous lifetimes.

To be fifteen forever, trapped in a feline's body with all those raging teenage hormones….

Maybe Galahad had a right to be a little grouchy.

As the cat lay down in the sunshine, Lucian crossed to the store's oak counter and put away the hammer. Earlier, he'd started sorting through a box of silverware his grandfather had bought at auction and stored until he had time to tag the pieces. As his grandfather had done before purchasing the lot, Lucian had confirmed by running his hand over the silver that none of the pieces held dark magic and therefore could be sold to the general public.

As Lucian set an ornate serving spoon on the counter, he thought of the gleaming cases of antique silver at the New England store. Until two months ago, he'd been the East Coast Representative for The Experts: a prestigious position. He'd screwed up, and had lost all that he'd worked for.

His jaw tightened on a flare of anger and disappointment while he tied the string of a white price tag around the spoon's handle.

"Now *there's* a lady I'd like to hear moan."

Lucian glanced up. A young woman wearing sunglasses stood outside the shop window, looking in.

He knew quite a few people in Cat's Paw Cove, but he didn't recognize her.

Wavy, blond hair brushed her bare shoulders. She wore a sleeveless white sundress, and as his gaze slid down her shapely curves, he saw the open cardboard box tucked under her left arm.

Was she a potential customer? Heat tingled in his gut; he hoped so.

"I saw her first," Galahad said, sounding petulant.

"True, but you're a cat."

To get a better look at Galahad, meowing and gazing up at her, she leaned closer to the window. The shift in posture brought the shadow of her cleavage into view. Lucian's hand curled against the counter's cool surface, for he longed to see more.

Reining in his stirring of interest, he forced his attention back to the silverware. She might be on her way to one of the other shops on the downtown street—not bringing items to his grandfather's store for a free evaluation. Lucian didn't want to be caught ogling, no matter how much her hourglass figure appealed to him. She might think him one of those antique dealer geeks who was starved for a woman's attention.

He wasn't starved. Single, yes. But, he'd never had a problem getting a date when he wanted one.

As he fastened a price tag around another piece

of silver, though, he couldn't resist looking at her again. Shifting the box, she tapped on the glass and smiled at Galahad, who promptly rose to all fours and stretched to the tip of his tail.

Show off.

The woman's smile widened with delight.

How lovely she looked—

As she cooed to Galahad and leaned down even farther, something in the box shifted. Panic swept her features, and her free hand flew to keep items from falling out. Her sunglasses slipped from her nose.

Before Lucian realized he'd sprung into motion, he was halfway to the door.

"You *would* play chivalrous knight to the rescue," Galahad groused.

"Of course." Lucian pulled the wooden door open. A small bell attached to it chimed, a musical sound against the noise of the cars driving by on the street.

As he stepped outside, ninety-nine-degree heat washed over him. In the air-conditioned store, it was easy to forget just how scorching it could be in Florida. A shock-like tingle also raced through him, a sign he'd passed through the magical barrier his grandfather had set up around the premises—added protection in case a wily Dealer of Darkness decided to infiltrate the shop, or any of the dark magic artifacts tried to cause trouble.

Lucian hurried to the young woman. She crouched on the sidewalk, her skirt brushing the dirty concrete, the box in front of her. With careful hands, she felt the newspaper-wrapped items, as though checking nothing was broken. In the brilliant sunshine, her hair looked even more golden.

Either she hadn't heard the door open, or she was too concerned about breakage for her to acknowledge him right away. Looking down at her, he found himself in the perfect position to see what had been denied to him before. The shadowed valley of her cleavage was framed by the lacy white trim of her bra—

No. He was a gentleman. He wouldn't ogle—

A thudding noise intruded: Galahad, up on his hind legs and pawing on the other side of the glass.

A timely interruption.

"Is everything all right?" As Lucian crouched beside the woman, he caught a hint of her citrusy perfume.

Her shoulders--slopes of fair, satiny skin—tensed. Either she was reluctant to answer his question, or she'd only just become aware of him. Her long lashes flickered then she looked up at him. Her blue-eyed gaze held his before she looked back down at the box. "Oh, damn it," she muttered.

Lucian's excitement fizzled. Most women, when he talked to them, smiled. Many tried to prolong the conversation with flirting and touching his arm. Not once had a woman answered him by averting her gaze and cussing.

"Sorry. I didn't mean to be rude." She peered down at the box again. "I lost one of my contact lenses yesterday. It went down the bathroom sink, and I haven't had a chance to buy more." Her hand slid to the right. "My sunglasses are prescription. I know they fell in here somewhere—"

"Bottom right corner," Lucian said, just as her fingertips hit the tortoiseshell plastic frames.

Her shoulders dropped on a relieved sigh. "Thank you."

"My pleasure."

She pushed the sunglasses onto the bridge of her nose. Perspiration glistened on her face, and Lucian suddenly became aware of the sweat trickling down the back of his neck and under the collar of his polo shirt.

Be a gentleman. Invite her in.

When she picked up the box and rose, he stood as well.

Their gazes met again. As though seeing him for the first time, a pretty blush stained her cheekbones. Her gaze darted over his shirt that fit snugly enough to show off the muscles he'd built through intense workouts at the gym—the only way he'd kept his sanity through the turmoil of the past few months.

"Well." She sounded a little breathless. "Thank you so much for your help."

Lucian ignored the *thud* of Galahad's paws on the window again. "It's very hot out here." Good God, could he not have come up with something more inspiring to say?

"Yes, it is." Her expression turned rueful. "It's supposed to be a heat index of one-hundred-and-five today. I'm not used to such temperatures or the humidity."

Was she was a visitor to Florida? To Cat's Paw Cove? He must find out.

As she wiped her brow with the back of her hand, Lucian managed his most charming smile. He gestured to the shop's open door. "Why don't you come in for a moment and cool off?"

Read the rest of Lucian and Molly's story in Catherine Kean's book *Hot Magic*, available Tuesday, December 10 in eBook and print.

About Catherine Kean

Award-winning author Catherine Kean's love of history began with visits to England during summer vacations, when she was in her early teens. Her British father took her to crumbling medieval castles, dusty museums filled with fascinating artifacts, and historic churches, and her love of the awe-inspiring past stuck with her as she completed a B.A. (Double Major, First Class) in English and History. She went on to complete a year-long Post Graduate course with Sotheby's auctioneers in London, England, and worked for several years in Canada as an antiques and fine art appraiser.

After she moved to Florida, she started writing novels, her lifelong dream. She wrote her first medieval romance, *A Knight's Vengeance*, while her baby daughter was napping. Catherine's books were originally published in paperback and several were released in Czech, German, and Thai foreign editions. She has won numerous awards for her stories, including the Gayle Wilson Award of Excellence. Her novels also finaled in the Next Generation Indie Book Awards, the National Readers' Choice Awards, and the International Digital Awards.

When not working on her next book, Catherine enjoys cooking, baking, browsing antique shops, shopping with her daughter, and gardening. She lives in Florida with two spoiled rescue cats.

Catherine loves to keep in touch with her readers! Please follow her on the following sites:

Website
www.catherinekean.com

Facebook
https://www.facebook.com/Catherine-Kean-Historical-Romance-Author-196336684235320/

BookBub
https://www.bookbub.com/profile/catherine-kean

Goodreads
https://www.goodreads.com/author/show/695820.Catherine_Kean

Amazon Page
https://www.amazon.com/Catherine-Kean/e/B001JOZEMU/

About Wynter Daniels

Bestselling author Wynter Daniels has written more than three dozen romances, including contemporary, romantic suspense, and paranormal romance books for several publishers including Entangled Publishing and Carina Press as well as for Kristen Painter's Nocturne Falls Universe.

In 2019, she started CPC Publishing with author Catherine Kean.

She lives in sunny Florida with her family and a rescue cat named Chloe (who thinks she is dog, and tries all day to distract Wynter from writing).

Wynter loves to keep in touch with her readers! Please follow her on the following sites:

Website
https://www.wynterdaniels.com/

Facebook
https://www.facebook.com/wynter.daniels

BookBub

https://www.bookbub.com/search?search=Wynter+
Daniels

Goodreads

https://www.goodreads.com/author/show/3521407.
Wynter_Daniels

Instagram

https://www.instagram.com/wynterdaniels/

Amazon Page

https://www.amazon.com/Wynter-
Daniels/e/B003U2KQCM/

Coming Tuesday, October 15
from Cat's Paw Cove

Artist Samantha Cartwright arrives in Cat's Paw Cove for a visit with her great Aunt Emma, hoping to get clarity about Emma's cryptic prediction. Instead, Sam finds out she must mind her aunt's metaphysical shop while Emma is away on vacation. The temporary job proves impossible for Sam because unlike Emma, Sam possesses no magical powers. Lucky for her, tall, dark, and handsome help enters the shop just in the nick of time.

Eli Kincaid managed to get on the bad side of a ruthless loan shark. Now his life depends upon his ability to con an innocent woman out of the only thing of value she owns—a precious jewel she inherited. If he can get close to Sam, maybe he can figure out where she's keeping the gem. What he hadn't counted on was falling for his mark. Can he escape the web of deception and protect Sam as sinister forces close in on both of them?

Available in eBook and print.

Coming Friday, November 1
from Cat's Paw Cove

Eight holiday tales set in the magical town of Cat's Paw Cove:

FAMILIAR BLESSINGS by Candace Colt
To repay an old man who brought him out of war's dark shadow, a former Army Ranger delivers a cryptic letter to a gifted medium in Cat's Paw Cove. If what the letter says is true, the reluctant medium and skeptical Ranger must travel back to 1720 to save a young boy from the gallows.

CHRISTMAS AT MOON MIST MANOR by Kerry Evelyn
Lanie and Matt Saunders return to Cat's Paw Cove two years after their first disastrous Christmas there. When a mysterious kitten leads Matt back in time, can he right the wrongs of the past and give his expectant wife the perfect Christmas?

CHARLOTTE REDBIRD: GHOST COACH by Sharon Buchbinder
With the help of hunky real estate agent, Dylan Graham, life coach Charly Redbird and her new kitten have found the perfect home next to a cemetery.

Charly gets a new client right away, who happens to be her neighbor—and a ghost. What could possibly go wrong?

GNOME FOR THE HOLIDAYS by Kristal Hollis
When an empath who's failed at every relationship impulsively kisses an enchanted garden gnome, he magically turns into a real man. Together they must find his one true love and end the curse by Christmas or he'll be forever alone and trapped within his stone prison.

RING MA BELL by Debra Jess
In 1979, Michael Bell fell in love with high seas radio technician Dvorah Levi's voice as she guided him to safety, but their marriage was cut short by a bullet. Forty years later, Dvorah still mourns him. Can a special holiday and a magical Sherwood cat bring him back?

PURRFECTLY CHRISTMAS by Mia Ellas
Faerie Sormey Johnson moved to Cat's Paw Cove to live a quiet life as a human until a sexy werewolf deputy needs her help tracking down a murderous monster. When Sormey offers herself as bait, the cost may be more than she bargained for.

COLLYWOBBLES FOR CHRISTMAS by Sue-Ellen Welfonder
The fate of star-crossed lovers falls into the magical paws of a time-traveling kitten determined to right an ancient wrong and claim the greatest Christmas gift of all - love.

NEW YEAR'S KISS by Darcy Devlon
In order to overcome a family curse, Griffin Brooks, the town's hotshot assistant fire chief, must earn his true love's trust. Trina Lancaster knows she can release Griffin's curse, but will her magical family baggage be a deal breaker?

Available in eBook and print.

Coming Tuesday, January 7, 2020
from Cat's Paw Cove

What if Mr. Right was really Mr. Wrong?

Former ugly duckling Sydney McCoy yearns to break into television. And the hottest guy she works with—TV sports personality, Chip Haggerty—could be her ticket to the airwaves. Too bad that Chip hardly knows Sydney is alive. Worse, she has no clue how to speak Chip's sports-oriented language.

Up-and-coming real estate agent Levi Barnett is desperate to convince the owner of a hot downtown property to sell so the company Levi works for can redevelop the site into a multi-million-dollar complex. When he literally crashes into a woman he knew in high school who could champion his cause, he'll do anything to get Sydney's help. All she wants from him in return is help communicating with her office crush. No problem! But when Levi starts to fall for the beautiful Sydney, he wonders if he's making the worst mistake of his life by being her would-be Cyrano de Bergerac.

Available in eBook and print.

Made in the USA
Lexington, KY
05 November 2019

56545749R00090